PRAISE FOR *TIME & CO*

"... a wonderfully entertaining, yet thoughtfully realistic coming of age [story] ... her actions wreak havoc ... and have the potential to utterly destroy ... her chances for success ... This is a tale of redemption that will resonate with readers of all ages, especially young adult readers who are themselves in the throes of navigating the complexities of life on their road to maturity."
— SHAREN E. MCKINNEY-ALSTON,
RETIRED PRINCIPAL, PROFESSOR & EDUCATOR

"... a great read! The story allows us to ... see ourselves or someone else we know. It's funny. It's serious. It moves us to search for solutions to our own dilemmas. The title is very appropriate for the way the majority of us live, whether we realize it or not."
— GAIL L. JOHNSON, RETIRED TEACHING
SUPERVISOR & EDUCATOR

"Having been a health care provider for over 30 years, working strictly by appointment, time management is crucially important. Respect for my patients' time and their respect for mine is the lifeblood that keeps our practice running smoothly. The lessons taught in Time & Consequences are of vital importance for young people to learn. Told in a story they can relate to, young readers of all ages will take away a lesson to live by, for all aspects of their personal and future professional lives. Thank you, M. Lauryn for getting the message out!"
— DAVID A. GREENE, D.D.S.

"All of us have specific experiences dealing with time. We try to manage it in increments to our advantage. Some of us are successful and some of us, not so much. Turquoise takes us on a journey of discovery—If we pay attention, we'll learn how to master time."
— MARVA GOINS, EDUCATOR & AUTHOR

"I would highly recommend the book *Time & Consequences* by M. Lauryn Alexander. The book impresses the reader with the importance of being punctual. It is a wonderful life skill that I as a teacher taught to students.

I had a former student who was constantly late and missed the first hour of school several times a week. Being late caused her to have a poor reading grade. I explained this to her father during a school conference. He was very receptive to having her come to school on time. She became very punctual and became a successful student. She is now a concert pianist."

— Michele Boyer, Retired Kindergarten Teacher

Time & Consequences was such a great read. It was an absolute mood lifter that will keep you laughing and wanting to read more and more. It also teaches life lessons without getting preachy. I highly recommended it to any teen.

— J. D. High School Student

"According to the psychotherapist, Stephanie Sarkis, "Time blindness is a difficulty with a perception of time, how much time is passed, and how much time it's going to take to do something". https://bitly.ws/34BeL. I am coping with time blindness myself and a friend of mine recommended that I should read *Time & Consequences*.

Much to my surprise, I realized that I had similar lateness habits as the main character in this book. Even though this is a fiction novel, in reality this problem can be a daily challenge in the real world. I'm glad that I've read this book and I am working hard on finding solutions for my tardiness. There is hope for people like me!"

— Rafael G. Lopez, College student
AND A MUCH-APPRECIATED READER

"As a dual career holder; timing is everything to me. Going from one job to another on a daily basis can be challenging. I have had a few subordinates who couldn't resonate with being timely in one career vs. two! My words of encouragement or support often fell on deaf ears. I ordered a few copies of this amazing book; which put time and the ramifications for not being timely into perspective for my employees. The lessons noted in this book are invaluable and I can't wait for it to reach more people with translations! The relatable story will stand the test of all time to come!"

"A life is not important except in the impact it has on other lives."
— *Jackie Robinson*

— Ayana Koné,
Assistant VP, Morgan Stanley

"I highly recommend *Time & Consequences* to anyone looking for an engaging and thought-provoking read. The novel brilliantly emphasizes the significance of punctuality and the long-term effects of our daily time-management decisions. Turquoise Nez Timerhorn's journey is a huge reminder that time is a precious and that should never be taken for granted. This book is a must-read for anyone seeking to improve their time-management skills and achieve their goals."

—Jerome Denobrega, Project Manager

TIME &
CONSEQUENCES

M. LAURYN ALEXANDER

SUCCESS
ESSENTIALS
PUBLISHING
COMPANY, INC.®

Published by
SUCCESS ESSENTIALS PUBLISHING COMPANY, Inc.®
1040 First Avenue, #142, New York, New York 10022-2991
www.TimeandConsequences.com

This publication is available at a special rate for bulk purchases for
educational, nonprofit, fund raising, or institutional needs. If interested,
please email Success Essentials Publishing Company Inc® at
Publish@PublishBySE.com.

This is a work of fiction. Names, characters, places, and incidents are
either the product of the author's imagination or are used fictitiously, and
any resemblance to actual persons, living or dead, business establishments,
events, or locales is entirely coincidental.

Printed in the United States of America

Revised Edition: 2023

Library of Congress Control Number: 2017900733

ISBN (paperback): 978-0-9907585-4-9
ISBN (eBook): 978-0-9907585-3-2

IN MEMORIAM

To the memories of my mother and father,
who were proactive in making sure that I received
the best education they could give me,
taught me about the important things in life,
and loved me unconditionally.

Acknowledgements

Collaboration (Noun) = the act of working together
to make or produce something.

— *Longman Dictionary of American English*
www.longman.com

The publishing of this book took almost twenty years and many hours of research. I am pausing now to thank several friends, professionals, and family members who have helped me to produce this literary work of realistic fiction.

Many people were supportive in diverse ways. First, I would like to thank Lynn Williams. Secondly, I would like to thank David A. Dobosz, a former educator, a true wordsmith without whom I could not have completed this novel. He was a lifelong friend.

Finally, there were several people who are no longer living who were incredibly supportive throughout these years.

It takes dedication and perseverance to achieve the pinnacle of any endeavor. The collaborative effort made this book possible.

Last, but not least, I want to thank all of you who have purchased this book.

DISCLAIMER

Eagles are birds that soar high above
mountains in the sky. They glide effortlessly
through the clouds. In our culture, we usually
don't describe an eagle as "running."

We use the idiomatic expression "I am running late"
to tell someone we will not be at our designated
location on time. Thus, using my privilege as a
writer, I have linked the words "Early Running
Eagle" in this context throughout this novel.

TIME &
CONSEQUENCES

M. LAURYN ALEXANDER

Table of Contents

The Journey Continues (Part II)

The Journey Endures (Part III)

THE JOURNEY BEGINS
(PART I)

1

Two Tickets to Happiness

Ed Windsong held two tickets to happiness tightly in his strong bronze fist. With much care, he slipped the tickets behind the crisp one-hundred-dollar bill that he kept in his smooth, brown leather wallet. The large bill was there only for an emergency. He had never felt the necessity to spend it.

Ed, a high school senior, felt he was the luckiest guy in the world. His 6' 1", 185-pound, muscular frame moved like a gazelle both on and off the basketball court. Most people mistook Ed for a Madison Avenue supermodel because of his above-average looks. But he was not a model. He was the powerhouse captain of an unbeatable high school basketball team, the Cranes.

Hawthorne Hills High School's best basketball player, Ed, had both the talent and the power to make or break anyone who got in his way on the court. Ed played to win. No one at Hawthorne Hills High School could remember a winning streak of this magnitude, 25-0. Ed's eagerness to emulate other great basketball stars made him a formidable opponent.

Having athletic prowess was not enough for Ed "The Scholarman." His academic average in school for all of his subjects put him in the top 5 percent of his graduating class. He had his eyes set on a scholarship to Kingsmith College. He planned to attend their law school after his undergraduate degree was completed. Negotiating contracts fascinated him immensely.

Ed brought this same passion to his relationship with a certain young lady. He could not imagine being without her. His fingers demanded that he pick up his cell phone. He had to have an answer about the two tickets in his pocket. He dialed her number — as he had countless times in the past, whether he was at home or at his part-time job.

It was a warm, late May afternoon in 2006 which was filled with expectations and hope. As a file clerk at the law offices of Bracy, Wong & Lopez, Ed enjoyed many perks at his part-time job. He did not earn enough money to carry around a sleek, black cellular phone in a burgundy leather briefcase — but he owned both of these things nonetheless. Some things, to his way of thinking, were essential to have in order to make a statement about who you were and where you were going in life.

"Good afternoon. May I please speak to Miss Timerhorn?" Ed spoke in a distinguished voice, like a newscaster from the six o'clock news.

"Hi, Edward, you must be calling from work, right?" teased the velvety voice on the other end of the line.

"Yeah — how did you know?" Ed said, chuckling to himself.

"You know my first name, and you didn't use it. You called me 'Miss Timerhorn.' That's a dead giveaway, if I ever heard one, Edward," quipped the young lady who had stolen Ed's heart with her analytical mind and intoxicating smile.

"Please call me 'Ed'," the masculine voice sternly pleaded.

"Let's not go there, Edward! You know I get great joy out of calling you 'Edward.' It might be because no one else does," laughed the taunting voice, ignoring the fact that it offended him. Turquoise felt that she could call him anything she wanted to. After all, her initials were "T.N.T.", pure dynamite.

In more formal situations, she was known as Turquoise Nez Timerhorn. She was a bronze bombshell with brains and a determined mind. The radiant smile that she flashed to everyone made them feel like she was speaking directly and exclusively to them — and them only. Everyone wanted to talk to her.

When people met Turquoise, they treated her like a celebrity. In turn, she treated them like a friend. Despite her parents' warning, "Don't talk to strangers," she had an unusually candid ability to instantly consider anyone she met her friend. She collected business cards from people and placed the person's name in her address book, filing these names under the category of "friend," even if she never saw the individuals again in her life.

Turquoise felt that she could communicate well with Edward — the nickname she tenderly called him by, even though his birth certificate had his name as "Ed Windsong." She never considered that calling someone by a name other than his or her given name was a form of manipulation.

With no response from Edward after ten seconds, Turquoise cleared her throat.

"Well, Edward, are we going or not?" asked Ed's girlfriend in an impatient, cooing voice.

She continued talking in her patented nonstop manner.

"Are we going to make our Senior Prom 'a night to remember'?"

Ed's mood softened and a grin spread across his face as he tried to conceal his romantic thoughts. "Yes, we are going to the Hawthorne Hills High School Senior Prom. I have just picked up our two tickets to happiness."

"To happiness?" mused Turquoise reflectively as she stared at her calendar on her wall. She saw that the prom was less than two weeks away. So much to do, so little time!

Momentarily, Ed dropped his voice to a soft, breezy whisper. "Just think, honey drop, a year and a half ago, this dream could not have been."

"Yes, Edward. I remember that fateful day when I spilled acid on your work shoes and briefcase in the chemistry lab."

"That I didn't mind, but what really bothered me was that your average was two points higher than mine," Ed laughed playfully. He touched the tarnished spot on his briefcase while he shook his head, saying, "I still carry around a tiny stain of your acid-love on my briefcase as a remembrance of you, baby-cakes," Ed teased in a phony "I'll-get-even with-you" voice.

"Hey, pumpkin, I'm the luckiest guy in the world to have such a gem like you."

"No, I'm lucky to have you," sighed Turquoise.

Ed hung up the telephone nine minutes later with the words, "I'll pick you up at six o'clock on prom night."

Becky

Turquoise never had to worry about finding dates. On the contrary, Ms. Timerhorn had complained on several occasions to her best friend Rebecca Córpuz about how many dates she had to turn down.

Four years ago, at the beginning of their freshman year of high school, she had commented to Rebecca, "They were all lovesick puppies, Becky."

"Gee, I wish I had your problem," Rebecca murmured under her breath that day as she bit her already short fingernails. As a recent immigrant to America, Rebecca always felt at odds with her new culture.

"Turquoise, can you tell me how you — eh, eh, er?" stammered Becky. She continued with her inquiry but this time with jerky speech, "Can you tell me how you make boys '*know-tiss u*'?"

Becky looked up to discover her question had fallen on absent ears. Her friend's silky long legs had carried her away to her next class. She was no longer at Becky's side.

Rebecca knew Turquoise as well as she knew herself. They had attended the same middle school and now high school together.

"Hi. What's your name?" an inquisitive girl sitting next to another classmate in Mrs. Jones's seventh-grade class on that cool September morning in 2000 had asked.

"Huh? Me?" responded a shy girl who pulled her fingers out of her mouth in order to reply to a bold classmate. After pausing for a second, the classmate replied, "I'm Rebecca Córpuz," the student answered in a barely audible voice.

For a brief moment, she glanced down at the floor and then faced the classmate, who apparently wanted to make friends with her. She continued the conversation and asked, "And what's yours?"

"I'm Turquoise Nez Timerhorn."

"That's a long name. What do your parents call you at home?"

"Just 'Turquoise' — but my older sister calls me 'T.N.T.' She teases me because my initials are the same as dynamite. Do you have a nickname?"

"'Rebecca' sounds too grown up for me, so I prefer to be called 'Becky.'"

"There you go. I'll call you 'Becky.'"

"Do you want to have lunch together later in the cafeteria?"

"Okay. Let's be quiet now, because Mrs. Jones is looking at us. We'll talk later."

And later they did talk. From the beginning of middle school, straight through their senior year in high school, these pals spoke daily by phone, studied at the local library, ate at each other's home, and went to the stores together every August for Back-to-School shopping. To know someone so well can be a blessing or a curse, because you know his or her *modus operandi*.

"Becky, I can't believe the prom is just around the corner," Turquoise mused.

"Yeah, and what am I going to do about my nails? It's a nervous habit. I just can't help it."

"Nobody's perfect. I've got my issues, too!"

Kismet had brought them together. Their mutual interests had blossomed into a true friendship.

3

Let the Decorating Begin

The Grand Ballroom of the Golden Paradise Hotel had been closed off for two days in order to prepare it for prom night. It was traditional for the prom to be held at this local architectural landmark. Its grand arches made kings and queens of the ordinary people who passed through its portals.

The Hawthorne Hills Prom Committee had started to transform the Grand Ballroom. Soon it would become a teenager's fantasy pavilion. The stage was being set as an elaborate throne room for the coronation of the royal couple who would become King and Queen.

As the last committee member walked into the ballroom, the festive mood began.

"It's 9:13 a.m.," said Paul Wyker to the students who had come to help set up, while he sipped his second cup of coffee. Feeling like a teenager again, Mr. Wyker announced to his volunteers, "Let's do it! Let the games — *Ooops* — I mean, let the decorating begin!"

As Student Activity Advisor to the high school seniors, Mr. Wyker adorned the walls with the first indigo and cream balloons. These were his favorite colors.

Mr. Wyker had never outgrown his love and excitement of being with young people. After teaching six years on the college level, he chose to return to his beloved Hawthorne Hills High School, from which he had graduated many years before.

As a young adult, Paul Wyker loved to party. Now, as the Student Advisor for a graduating class of 388 seniors, he had his hands full, playing surrogate father, advisor, minister, and handyman to the senior class.

He knew what it took to make a prom. After all, he had supervised and emceed proms for twenty-two consecutive years. He was always proud to be the one to surprise the crowd by announcing the royal couples.

These coveted titles, along with the publicity, would highlight the evening for any senior lucky enough to be chosen. The entire student body had to validate one choice and an alternate for each title, just in case the King or Queen might be disqualified. However, in the entire history of the school, no one could remember any alternates actually winning the crowns.

My Girl

The humid air made people walk slower than usual to their homes. It was dusk. The day before the Hawthorne Hills High School prom held many hopes.

Four tall figures walked in the waning light. One pair was identical except that one threw the basketball with his strong right hand, while the other one had exceptional shooting skills using his left.

One solo figure trailed behind them. The loner took firm steps to catch up with the other guys, who were a few paces ahead of him.

"Hey, you benchwarmers!" yelled Ed Windsong aloud, prankishly. The 230-pound, 6' 10" muscular frame of Griffin Lee Browne stopped dead in his tracks. He slowly turned halfway around. Instantly he flexed a big fist at the sorry sucker who dared to yell such a ridiculous insult at him.

"Hey, my fist fits right in yer bloody mouth," barked Griffin until he turned fully around toward Ed. "What's up?" Griffin said as he greeted his good buddy, the captain of his basketball team, the Cranes.

It irked Griffin that Ed met life in such a relaxed and casual way. Everything seemed to fall into place for the team's captain so naturally — his athletic talent *and* friendship with Turquoise. Griffin asked himself regularly, "Why do I let him get to me the way I do?"

"Hey, guy. Aren't you listening to me? Do you hear me?" Ed asserted as he interrupted Griffin's thoughts, which showed as a glazed look on his face. "You're my friend, Griffin, and my teammate."

"My man, we work like a charm both on and off the court," bragged Griffin as he shook his head to recover himself. He looked directly into Ed's eyes and stated, "Watch me score more points than you do off the court. You just don't know who the lucky one is." Griffin jeered at his team captain.

The previous basketball season had made enormous headlines in local and regional newspapers. Both Ed and Griffin enjoyed the fame, and no one took home the blame. Coach Aponte's two-line speeches still rang loud and clear in the ears and hearts of these two rival teammates.

Ed, Griffin, Jonathan Quincy, Colón Benitez, and his mirror-image twin-brother Victor were joking and jesting with each other about the tuxedos the young men would wear.

"Colón Benitez and Becky Córpuz are a pair for tomorrow evening," announced Colón, the 6' 5" small forward of the Cranes.

Ed joked, "Who comes first — C.B. or B.C.?"

"Colón Benitez is on court first, before my sweetheart, Ms. Rebecca Córpuz," Colón laughed to Ed. He was proud to be the skilled right-handed small forward on the Cranes team.

He and everyone else knew that Becky was the center of his off-court life. However, Colón wondered, from time to time, if their relationship was all too predictable. Colón and Becky had become an inseparably charming couple. Colón, from the Caribbean, and Becky, from the Philippines, had discovered their mutual ability to speak Spanish, and they explored the many ways their respective cultures were both similar and distinct.

To compete with his brother, Victor Benitez, the left-handed power forward, abruptly spoke up, "I'm not telling you who I'm bringing to the prom."

Victor was an independent spirit. He joined the crew when he felt like it.

"Ms. Natasha Orlov is my date," chimed in Jonathan Quincy, the 6' 6" shooting guard for the Cranes basketball team. "I know that my girl, 'Tasha,' is going to be eye-catching. Plus, when a tune suddenly flashes into her mind, her voice gives me chills. I can't wait for you to hear her perform at the prom."

Meanwhile, Griffin tempted the other guys with his female friend who *does more.*

"I scored the best. My date is Valerie Dewmore," taunted Griffin Lee Browne as he swaggered away, bragging over his left shoulder.

It had been half-time at an away game during their junior year. Valerie, the captain of the cheerleading squad, did a round off into a full split. Griffin was mesmerized. Little did he know that she had done it for him.

As they were boarding the bus for the trip back home, Griffin spied a seat next to Valerie. It was occupied by her pom-poms. Griffin asked her, "May I?" motioning toward the seat. Valerie responded with a nod, "Certainly!" tossing her hair lightly. It was history from there on.

The four basketball friends started to walk in opposite directions, but before they could get very far, Ed exclaimed, "Wait! Don't you want to know who 'my girl' will be?" They had already suspected what name was coming. As they awaited Ed's announcement, Griffin locked gazes with his team's captain. Ed boasted, "I have a date with Miss T.N.T. herself."

In miraculous unison, the five basketball players blurted out "Turquoise Nez Timerhorn."

Griffin turned away swiftly from Ed. His resentment toward Ed and Turquoise's relationship was strategically hidden under a mask of friendship. He ordered his pounding heart to calm down. It obeyed. In his mind, Griffin had mistaken Turquoise's friendly smile for flirtation. Griffin craved approval.

He told himself silently, *"Don't overreact. Your day will come."* Griffin walked away ... and waited ... and watched.

Biology

It was now almost two years since a certain young lady had brought a blush to Griffin's face, which sported a well-trimmed goatee. It was their sophomore year. Both students were lab partners in Mr. Gary Samuel's biology class.

Griffin's gift of gab had always impressed the girls — all except one. Around her, he was speechless. Griffin carefully orchestrated a campaign to win Turquoise's heart by staying up half of the night studying. Then he would show off his intellectual prowess in class by answering as many questions as possible in the biology class. He would first clear his throat to emphasize the fact that a response to a question was forthcoming. Turquoise often heard Griffin's bass voice trumpet the right answers in class.

One day, Turquoise said to him during the bio lab, "Griffin, my muffin, can you help me dissect this poor little piglet?" Just the sound of her voice would turn Griffin's personality from normal to numb. Then Griffin's bravado went down in flames.

Griffin's reputation as a ladies' man faded from player to love-struck admirer of Turquoise. Griffin memorized everything about her. He knew the scent of her perfume and the deep, sultry sound of her voice. Turquoise was a rare treasure.

His fixation on Turquoise grew each passing day like weeds popping up in a garden of an imaginary conquest.

One day after class, Griffin boldly spoke to the only one whom he regarded as worthy of being his girl.

"Hi ya, Turquoise. I see you got another ninety-nine on Mr. Samuel's biology test."

"You didn't do so bad yourself, Griffin, my muffin."

Turquoise's alluring voice made Griffin gush. She giggled softly and looked up toward Griffin's massive right shoulder. She said, "Now I'll have to call you 'Mr. One Hundred.'" She gently tapped Griffin on his right shoulder to recognize her classmate's achievement.

"Congratulations, Griffy!" she said to the young man who already had a Mount Everest-sized crush on her.

Griffin's massive frame made him an awesome force both on and off the basketball court — except when he was with Turquoise. His major goal was to get a date with Turquoise. Up until now he had fouled out every time.

At the end of the school year, Griffin and Turquoise passed their biology regents and class. Now the challenge was on in their junior year in high school.

But, at the end of Griffin's sophomore year, a new force had emerged. Ed Windsong transferred from a private high school in his junior year to Hawthorne Hills. The champion Cranes basketball team had gained another shining star, according to Coach Al "Winn-It-All" Aponte. "Winn" was the coach's middle name.

Ed "The Scholarman" Windsong was smart, with drop-dead good looks. Ed, the point guard, had it all. His way with words made him able to turn a bad situation into a better one. Without trouble, he easily became the new kid on the block and enjoyed meeting new faces during his junior year.

Griffin's ability to capture a date with Turquoise dwindled as Ed's influence on Turquoise increased. Turquoise never quite realized that Griffin was madly in love with her. After all, Turquoise used her charisma on everyone.

One day, Griffin was standing alone in the gym locker room at school after a grueling game and vowed, "Watch out, world. I am Griffin Lee Browne."

As he left the building, Griffin heard his new rally cry echo inside his head. "It's not over yet, my lady luck. Not by a long shot! I thought you would already be in my arms and not in the arms of Windsong," he grumbled to himself. The only solace he could find at that moment was that he was still the strongest center on the court.

The honk of a car horn had brought him back to the present. He had reached home by autopilot. He said under his breath, "There will be upcoming games to show off my 'on court skills' as well as off-court opportunities. No one beats me!"

6

What About Me?

Coach Aponte recalled the ups and downs of his two star players during their junior year. After several intense arguments had broken out about game strategies during the junior year, Coach Aponte warned his two best players, in the locker room, about their rivalry on the basketball court. He knew that their egos were bigger than the Grand Canyon and reminded them that he was their coach. He was the one calling the final shots! "In spite of all this drama, we're still winning," Coach Aponte consoled himself.

Nevertheless, Coach Aponte felt compelled to speak to Ed and Griffin like the sons he never had. Throughout their junior and senior years, Coach Al had noticed the two friends' increasing tension during those last few championship seasons.

However, after another serious altercation broke out between Ed and Griffin during February of their senior year,

Coach Aponte discovered the likely provocation behind these clashes.

After a winning game, Coach Aponte had zoomed in on a foursome who troubled him. With the Cranes behind by a point and with time running out, Griffin threw caution to the wind and hard-pressed the ball down the court. With just a few seconds left, he shot from the top of the key to make a three-point basket. The crowd erupted in applause. The risk had paid off. But after the buzzer sounded, Ed approached Griffin and shook an apparently critical finger at Griffin as if to say, "You didn't follow the play." Simultaneously, Valerie and Turquoise rushed to the floor toward the players, followed closely by the cheering squad and the rest of the Cranes team who had been on the bench. As the young lady in fuchsia brushed past Griffin, his eyes followed her in disbelief. Ed hoisted Turquoise into the air in jubilant celebration.

Completely ignoring Valerie's attempt to do the same for him, Griffin threw his palms up in an obvious gesture — "What about me?" as his jaw dropped dejectedly and he slunk off the court. Flabbergasted, Valerie could only watch in disgust.

The day before the last game, which would determine the division championship, Coach Aponte ordered both players to remain in the locker room as the rest of the team was leaving. Thinking primarily about how to win the championship for Hawthorne Hills High School, Coach Al took desperate measures and went beyond his role as a coach.

He stopped for a split-second to reflect on the rivalry between Ed and Griffin. Suddenly he heard the double-barrel thunder outside, *Boom-Boom* — like the threatening blows of two prize fighters in combat. The coach knew that neither the championship nor winning the respect and love of one young lady could become a reality through cutthroat competition.

The memory of his own heart-wrenching breakup with Olga — the result of his preoccupation with basketball — lashed into his mind. It reminded the coach that competition linked to a young man's ego could destroy relationships both on and off the court. Rivalry could blind a person to the real value of lifelong friendships between both teammates and young ladies. It could also ruin the mature collaboration needed to win in both sports and love.

Coach Aponte spoke frankly to Ed and Griffin at the same time. "Young men," he began. "Be very careful, or you'll lose something much more than you bargained for. You might win the game but forfeit something far more precious to each of you."

Coach Aponte's words thumped into the ears of Ed and Griffin. His words were permanently lodged in their minds, like guided missiles. The words had landed on target, never to be forgotten.

As the threesome left the gym to go their separate ways, two lightning bolts sliced the sky. As Coach Al dashed to his car in the downpour, he contemplated, "May the right man win the heart of the girl with the enticing smile."

7

Shop 'til You Drop

The sun peeked above the horizon as Turquoise rolled over for the first time in her bed. She was in the middle of a dream about her prom preparation.

On this early June 1st morning at 505 Silver Saddle Road, a tough but firm voice said, "Wake up, Turquoise — it's your prom day. Wake up, little one," said the voice — a voice that Turquoise had first heard when she was still in her mother's womb.

"I'll get up soon, Mom. I promise you," said Turquoise with a quiet protest.

"You have a one o'clock appointment at the beauty salon," reminded Teal Timerhorn as she opened the curtains to allow the bright sunlight into the room. "It is now 9:13 a.m." Teal had taken a vacation day to help her daughter prepare for the prom.

Turquoise's dream was just picking up speed. She turned over in bed for the second time and moved to turn off the alarm clock. She told herself that she would get up soon. *Ah, aarah, phew* — "I need just five more minutes of sleep. Yeah. Just five more minutes of sleep. Then, I can do battle for the day," Turquoise sleepily reassured her semiconscious mind.

As she turned for the third and final time under her two pillows, a soft murmur escaped from her mouth: "Yes, yes, yes. Just five more m-m-m— z-z-z— ooh-m-m — back to slumber — la-la — land."

Concurrently, the rest of the crew was eating breakfast together at their favorite hangout.

"Who do you think they are going to pick tonight?" Colón Benitez asked Becky.

"I don't know … but I do know that it has to be someone cool … you know … er — er … someone who can profile the glamorous look," explained Becky Córpuz.

Upon hearing Benitez's question, Griffin raised his voice, as if he was trying to speak over the noise of a landing plane. He intruded boldly from across the table, "Me."

Jonathan was quick to react by shaking his head with a smile.

"You don't have enough glamour, Griffin. My money is on Valerie."

"Who? Who? What did you say?" quickly inquired Griffin.

"You know," Jonathan said provocatively, "your date for the evening — the lovely Ms. Valerie Dewmore."

"Well, thank you for your vote of confidence," Valerie purred as she accepted Jonathan Quincy's verbal nomination for being crowned the Queen of the prom.

"Tasha, honey, can you pass me the ketchup?" requested Jonathan.

"Here you are, my luv," Natasha responded to her prom date, Jonathan Quincy, her black belt karate expert who made her feel safe when she was out with him.

Ed had been patiently waiting to join the conversation. With feigned formality, he announced, "Ladies and gentlemen. Please allow me to present my choice for Queen of the prom, Ms. Turquoise Timerhorn."

Meanwhile, back at the Timerhorn house, Turquoise was dashing around to get herself ready to leave at 11:00 a.m. She knew that it took thirty minutes to travel by train to the mall in downtown Brooklyn, New York.

But Turquoise, running late, left her house at 12:15 p.m. still confident that she'd make her 1:00 p.m. hair-salon appointment. Upon arriving at the mall at 12:45 p.m., she stumbled upon a sale at her favorite clothes store, *Michele's.*

"I'll take just a few minutes before my hair appointment to look around inside. Then I can run across the mall in three seconds and be at Margaret Blazer's Hair Salon on time."

Submerging herself into the world of shopping, she tried on several outfits. She hadn't gone shopping since she'd bought her prom dress a month ago. After she had tried on one more body-hugging dress, she made her decision. She would buy her namesake — a form-fitting silk turquoise dress that punctuated her graceful stride with a six-inch slit on the left side of the dress. Turquoise thought to herself, *I have a pair of stiletto heels that will look great with this dress.*

Turquoise imagined how the supple-silk turquoise dress would feel against her skin. She daydreamed about it for a few minutes and then returned to her present surroundings. She saw herself in the full-length mirror in the corner of the store. Her caramel complexion and her thick, raven hair complemented the dress.

While she was waiting on line to pay for her dress, she looked at the clock on the wall. It said 1:45 p.m. In disbelief, she looked at her own watch to double-check the time.

"No, no, no!" said Turquoise, as she realized that she would arrive more than forty-five minutes late for her hair-salon appointment. She hurriedly paid for the dress. Without considering the crowd of customers who were entering the clothing store, she shoved her shopping bag containing the unnecessary purchase against several women as she made her hasty escape.

8

Respect & Consequences

"Cool your jets, Turquoise. I know you think that I can rip and roar, wash and style your hair in a New York minute," scolded Margaret Blazer, the hair stylist, to the client who had arrived more than an hour late for her appointment.

"Have a seat. I'll fit you in between my other appointments."

Turquoise had no option but to wait. Margaret's unique skills in fashioning precision hair styles had won her many beauty awards. In Turquoise's mind. Margaret was worth the wait. She was angry with herself for wasting her precious prom-prepping time at the boutique, *shopping.*

It was 5:00 p.m. at the Golden Paradise Hotel, and the faculty chaperones were arriving. The hotel catering staff was putting their final touches on the table and banquet setups for their sumptuous prom dinner. The DJ and his band were also setting up their equipment.

At the very same time, a subway train conductor was announcing, "There is a sick passenger on the train. We will be delayed temporarily."

"I can't believe this is happening to me," muttered a fed-up Turquoise on her way home from the hair salon. Distressed at being more than three hours late, Turquoise couldn't contain her disappointment.

"I should be home getting ready for my big night. I got both my hair and nails done at last. This isn't cool," moaned Turquoise.

The woman next to Turquoise on the train shook her head. She noticed that the passenger next to her was muttering incessantly to herself.

The stranger thought, *This is how it can start. First, the talking out loud to oneself; next, the prescriptions come. Finally, life will never be the same after these episodes.* She quickly glanced over her shoulder at the pretty young woman again to confirm her suspicions.

Two minutes later, the train lurched forward. The sympathetic passenger got up from her seat. Taking a business card from her purse, she placed it into Turquoise's lap. She waited at the door and exited at the next stop.

In her attempt to pick up the card, Turquoise's many packages and bags spilled onto the floor of the train car. The train was again in motion. She sighed in relief that maybe, just maybe, she might not be too late for the prom.

Now, she had the opportunity to turn her attention to the business card that the strange woman had dropped in her lap. It read:

Tynna Isadora Arevalo, M.D.

Psychiatrist
On call 24 hours

Blakeville Counseling Center
260 Gateway Boulevard
Suite 452
Brooklyn, New York 11200
(347) 570-0001

Specializing in Chronic Compulsive Disorders

Across town Ed jumped and touched the ten-foot ceiling in the foyer of his home with his hand. His joyful spirit was looking forward to this special evening with an extraordinary young lady. He smoothed his tuxedo again. His strong slender fingers adjusted the bow tie for the last time. Looking forward and never turning back, Ed glanced at the watch on his left wrist. He acknowledged silently, *"Right on time."*

Sabera Windsong handed the corsage to her son as she beamed with pride. Although Ed had to work to have the money to purchase the things most high school boys needed, he was still able to excel academically. During Ed's brief free time, he and his father, Ben, would love to play a pick-up game of basketball at the local park. This, too, paid off. Ed was offered a full scholarship to both Kingsmith College and Hanford University.

"Make sure you take plenty of pictures," Sabera directed.

"And give the Timerhorns our best," added Ben Windsong.

He swung the front door of his home open with one hand. Destiny would close it for him — with a backhand.

As he walked on the tree-lined streets on his way to Turquoise's house, Ed enjoyed the scent of the fresh-cut grass. Without a care in the world, he headed to his sweetheart's house.

He glanced at his watch again and shortly arrived at the front door of his girlfriend's one-family home exactly at 5:45 p.m.

He rang the bell.

Teal Timerhorn greeted him with a grim look on her face. Being a native New Yorker, Ed took one look at her expression and imagined the worst.

"I'm sorry, Ed ..." Teal started to say.

Immediately, Ed's thoughts started spinning on a merry-go-round of tragedies.

"Is she injured? What hospital is Turquoise in? Was she kidnapped?" Ed inquired. "How much is the ransom?" Ed interrogated Turquoise's mother.

"No, no, no, Ed, calm down. She hasn't returned from her prom preparation yet," Mrs. Timerhorn said.

"Just have a seat, young man," Roy Timerhorn said in an authoritative tone from inside the living room.

Reluctantly, Ed walked into his girlfriend's home.

Teal told Ed that she would put the corsage in the fridge. She smiled and retreated to the kitchen. A few moments later, she reentered the living room, praying that her daughter could extricate herself from the hot water she was drowning in. A quick smile wouldn't fix this mess.

Ed gazed at Mrs. Timerhorn's smile as she strolled back from the kitchen. *The physical resemblance of mother and daughter was uncanny — thick, shiny, dark long hair and radiant smiles,* Ed thought to himself.

He sat down cautiously on the love seat. It allowed him to see anyone who entered or left the house. It also allowed him to peek through the curtains draped in front of the window. Ed waited patiently, but he found himself reflecting back on an earlier occasion when Turquoise had also kept him waiting.

It was less than a year ago, when he and Turquoise were to have a romantic dinner out at a nearby neighborhood restaurant. As Ed waited outside of the restaurant for Turquoise, he mused to himself, "Some things are worth waiting for — such as love and friendship." Then the words of Jeremy Taylor, a fifteenth-century British clergyman came to mind "Love is friendship set on fire."

Ed inhaled and exhaled before continuing with his silent, private thoughts on Turquoise's pattern of lateness.

Ed thought to himself, *Love has multiple levels. Love first starts out as a friendship. As it deepens, it can grow. However, when love is set aflame, it has intensity and passion.*

Thirty minutes had elapsed before Turquoise suddenly appeared at the restaurant. Her radiant smile, along with a quick kiss on Ed's left cheek, completely distracted his thoughts. All was forgotten — for the moment.

Ed, being a courteous gentleman, chose to temporarily ignore these early-warning signs. Instead, he pursued the love of his life.

After dinner, Turquoise asked, "Wasn't the food delicious?"

"Yes, Turquoise. It reminded me of the wonderful, home-cooked meals either of our mothers could have prepared for our families at home. By the way, Turquoise, I was waiting for you. I asked you to meet me at ..."

"Edward! I'm here with you now, and we have just shared a great meal and evening together. What is the point you are trying to make?"

"If our relationship means anything to you, sweetheart, you've got to respect it by arriving on time.

"Yes, Edward. Perhaps you're right. I realize that I need to plan my time better."

"I really hope that you do, because sometimes I worry that you don't fully understand how it affects others. The consequences may not be what you wish."

Now this recollection and conversation resurfaced as fresh wounds. Ed began to tap his right foot every three seconds, attempting to contain his disappointment and irritation.

Ed impulsively paced over to the window and glanced at his watch. It was 6:10 p.m. Thoroughly agitated, he turned on his heels and returned to his seat.

At exactly 6:15 p.m., the doorbell rang. Ed's heart did a lay-up shot. It began to beat faster with each stride that

Mr. Timerhorn took toward the door. Ed was hoping beyond hope that Turquoise would suddenly appear and that they might still make it to the prom on time.

Ed jumped up from the love seat to see who was at the front door. Stampeding past Mr. Timerhorn, he turned the brass knob.

Ed pulled the door open. He heard, "I am here to drive Mr. Windsong to the prom whenever he and the Junior Miss are ready to leave." It was Andrew "Zippy" Malone, the designated driver for this evening. The freshly waxed, black stretch limousine's motor was purring in front of the Timerhorns' house. Ed gave an order to the limousine driver, "Wait for me in the limo."

Zippy touched his navy blue chauffeur's hat with a quick salute to the brim. He turned his 5' 6" diminutive frame on his heels and hurried back to the limo.

"Relax, Ed. Go sit down, or I will have to give you a tranquilizer so that you don't tackle me at the front door again," advised Mr. Timerhorn, laboring for the correct words to calm down his daughter's prom date. *My lovely daughter has really made a mess of things this time*, thought Roy.

At 6:35 p.m., the waiting chauffeur sensed that something was amiss but couldn't put his finger on it. While Zippy sat behind the wheel of the limousine, he saw a tornado-like figure rumbling toward 505 Silver Saddle Road.

Zippy knew enough about human anatomy to know that the dark shadow was a Junior Miss. However, he could barely discern the faint mumbling as the dasher whizzed by his lowered limousine window, "… ever outrun time?"

9

What Will It Take?

At precisely 6:42 p.m. the sparks of a Fourth of July ignited inside the Timerhorns' home. Turquoise dashed through the door. Her shopping bags dropped to the living room floor.

"Mom? Dad? I'm home. You'll never guess wha-ta, wha-ta, hapin-happenin tu-tu-tuya meya-mm-me ..." Turquoise stammered and stuttered about her subway ordeal.

She gazed straight ahead into three pairs of accusative eyes on stoic faces. The controlled, shallow breathing alerted her that danger was in the air. Turquoise closed her eyelids halfway to spot the two tickets that Edward was holding in his clenched fist.

The couple was standing only two feet apart, yet their thoughts were immeasurably distant from each other. They were more like a pair of mismatched socks than two kids madly in love with each other.

Turquoise was in cut-off jeans and a torn red T-shirt. Ed's tuxedo was outfitted with a bright-red bow tie. *And they were both seeing red.*

Ed and Turquoise realized that she had been caught in an unforgivable act.

Turquoise blinked several times. She thought to herself, *I've never seen Ed this upset before. He is unbelievably silent.*

Turquoise flashed her famous smile, anyway.

"I couldn't help it," she pleaded as her smile faded into a pained expression.

Ed turned his head away from Turquoise's momentarily to gather more composure. Turning back to Turquoise, face to face, the frown across his forehead was obvious. Turquoise again attempted her most powerful weapon. She gave Ed a most dazzling grin.

It didn't work this time, either.

Sensing Ed's outrage, Turquoise backed away slowly. The palms of both her hands began to break out in an icy sweat. Sheepishly, Turquoise excused herself from the living room.

With the quick, tortured comment, "I'll be ready in fifteen minutes," Turquoise reassured Ed as she bolted up the stairs.

Flinging her day's purchases on the bed, she smudged one of her freshly painted nails in her rush. Taking inventory of the day's activities, she turned on a small fan and aimed it at her still slightly damp fingernails. They complemented her dove-white prom dress.

"Can I really be ready in fifteen minutes?" Turquoise rambled on to herself. "I'd better look good. That's my main objective now."

After the nail-drying session had ended, Turquoise slid into the bathtub of sweet-smelling bubble-bath water, scented like fresh-cut rosebuds.

A few strands of her hair got wet. "*Oops!* I don't want this to ruin the beautiful hairdo that Margaret Blazer created."

"I've got to look good," she repeated in order to bolster her confidence to face Edward again. She bathed faster than usual, concerned with the ticking of the clock, minute by minute.

Out of her bath, Turquoise was now lost in her own thoughts.

"What will it take for me to regain Ed's trust?"

10

Two Hands Are Better Than One

At 7:05 p.m., Teal knocked at Turquoise's bedroom door. Teal entered with the words, "Let's see if we can't get you out of here in the next few minutes."

"Thanks, Mom. I guess I need help tonight"

Teal wrapped a towel around Turquoise's shoulders and proceeded to apply her makeup.

"Honey," Teal began. "You know that this evening is a very special event for both you and Ed. The fact that you are so late is going to put a damper on your relationship. He is trying to make this occasion very memorable. Your natural charm will not be sufficient enough to overcome his profound disappointment."

Teal's advice continued, "Make sure that your attention is focused on Ed. You need to reassure him that his effort is not in vain. Show him that you appreciate being his date. With all the difficulties your lack of punctuality has caused, for you and others, you still have very redeeming and commendable interests and sensitivities."

Turquoise spotted the calendar with pictures of protected and endangered species above the clock on her wall. As her mother was applying eye shadow, she continued, "The time you spend volunteering at the animal shelter and youth center shows you have a large capacity for caring about others. This is what Ed is hoping to feel more of, in your relationship. Your lack of punctuality is sending him the message that you don't care."

With her makeup completed, Turquoise, assisted by Teal, put her stunning gown carefully over her shoulders. When her outfit was fully adjusted, Teal snapped on the silver necklace on Turquoise. It had several thin silver strands with one large gem as the centerpiece. It had a delicate inlay of black onyx, with accents of amethyst and turquoise stones in it. This special necklace had been a gift from her Edward. This unique and exquisite piece of jewelry was a Windsong family heirloom.

"M-m-m-m — thanks, Mom," Turquoise puckered up her full, shapely lips. The upper part of her hair was swept up halfway on top of her head with a silver hair ornament. The lower portion of her hair cascaded like a graceful, yet grand Niagara Falls around her shoulders, accentuating her off-the-shoulder gown, with curls bouncing around her lovely cheeks.

Ushering her out of the bedroom, Teal paused as Turquoise quickly snatched her favorite gemstone watch, designed by

D. Blackfoot & Company. It was the perfect complement to her necklace.

A quick assessment of the social damage led Turquoise to say quietly to herself, "I'm feeling good and looking good, but, oh, no-o-o-o — I'm so late!" As she finally reached the bottom stairs, would anything about her appearance make any difference now?

11

What Should I Do?

It was 8:00 p.m. at the Golden Paradise Hotel, and Mr. Wyker nodded approvingly at the assembled crowd. However, he was not as blasé as he seemed. The dinner service had been completed and the last remaining china was being removed. "I can't hold this ceremony off much longer," he argued to himself slamming shut his gold-plated pocket watch.

Mr. Wyker's thoughts were interrupted by a student's statement. "Hey, Mr. Wyker, how long are you going to wait before you give me my crown?" boasted arrogantly the second-best player on the Cranes basketball team.

"Griffin, young man, let's do it the democratic way. The voting ballots will name the King and Queen," responded Mr. Wyker.

Griffin swaggered back over to Ms. Valerie Dewmore and began to dance with her. He rubbed his cheek against the long rhinestone earring on her left ear. He whispered, "Val,

I've never seen you lovelier than you are tonight!" She kissed him on the cheek and held him even tighter.

Seconds later, the rest of the couples had lost track of how unusually late Ed was with Turquoise, as they danced to a hot salsa beat by a popular Hispanic singer.

"Sh-sh-sh, please," one of the chaperones asked of the students on the dance floor, "Paul Wyker wants our attention."

"It's time to announce the King and Queen of the prom," Mr. Wyker, the senior advisor, exclaimed to the enthusiastic crowd.

Each heart in the Grand Ballroom beat a little faster. Each person secretly wished that his or her name would be the one called by Mr. Wyker.

After twenty-two years of announcing the titles of King and Queen of the prom, the entertaining Paul Wyker had planned on using his stock repertoire of routine jokes to amuse this prom crowd. But destiny had dealt Paul a cruel hand tonight.

He knew what the students did not. It was time to announce the King and Queen of the evening, but they had not yet arrived. "What should I do?" pondered Mr. Wyker.

12

Cold Shoulder

An arctic wall now froze the affection Ed had previously felt toward Turquoise. Unspoken words boiled beneath the surface, waiting for a virtual guillotine to drop. The twenty minutes of silence felt endless, especially to Turquoise. They had traveled more than fifteen minutes from her home in the limousine without a smile from Ed.

Sitting on opposite sides in the back seat of the black limousine, Turquoise calculated her next move, like a Grand Master chess player. She noticed the full bar. It was filled with her favorite pink lemonade, a television, and two CD players with an assortment of musical selections. Turquoise thought to herself, *Wow! My Edward went to a lot of trouble to make this evening a happy one for the two of us.*

Instinctively, Turquoise moved an inch closer to Ed, who was gazing out the dark-tinted glass of the limousine.

"How do I look, Edward?" Turquoise asked flirtatiously, with a hint of timidity.

Ed tossed his girlfriend a flash of disgust and turned back to the window. Turquoise did not yet fully realize how deep a wound her lateness, this evening, had burned into Ed's heart. "How do I look, Edward?" Turquoise haplessly repeated.

At last, Zippy broke the one-sided icy stillness with his friendly words: "You look lovely, junior miss." Then, as a signal of decorum, he raised the limo's glass partition to give the couple their privacy.

Turquoise ignored the limo driver's compliment. Then she slid three inches closer toward Ed — who was acting more like "The Iceman" than "The Scholarman." Turquoise pretended to clear her throat with a gentle cough before speaking again.

"E-m-m– Em-m-m, Edward, I asked you a question," inquired Turquoise with an even tone in her best velvety voice.

Still no response! A brave Turquoise slid completely over the leather car seat to Ed's side. Turquoise's heart told her that, if she got closer, Ed might talk to her. She foolishly thought to herself, *Maybe the fragrance of my favorite perfume, Jeanine, might melt his heart, and he'll wrap his arms around me for my usual hug.*

Not able to take the tension any longer, Turquoise looked directly at Ed's handsome face as she hesitantly moved his head to face hers and then demanded, "Edward, do you hear me?" her voice rising an octave higher than normal.

The empty silence engulfed the couple like the vacuum of outer space.

Unexpectedly, without yelling a word, Ed finally released his pent-up frustration and anger. "Why did we have to be so late?" said Ed in a low voice.

"Turquoise, I arrived at your house before 6:00 p.m. The limousine driver arrived at 6:15 p.m." Ed blurted out in an aggrieved voice to his prom date. Closing his eyelids slightly to deliver the challenging question Ed asked, "Where were you?"

Both his expression and Ed's harsh cross-examination triggered an immediate withdrawal from Turquoise. Mumbling to herself, she slunk back to the other side of the limo, realizing for the first time that her beauty and schmoozing were useless. Ed had every right to be as upset as he was. Her lateness was inexcusable, especially on this evening.

Ed had accidentally pushed the two-way intercom button. Zippy was party to the agonizing conversation going on in the back of his limousine. Zippy kept his steel-blue eyes forward, never flinching at what he heard.

"Windsong is a man much like me," pondered Zippy. As he waited for the next green light, the chauffeur-turned-Indianapolis-500-Speedway driver meditated briefly. "Mr. Windsong puts a lot of value on being on time. Time is precious and should be treated with the utmost respect," philosophized Zippy.

Zippy's fast-paced, on-the-job education included a PhD in the Humanities from The Street Academy of Life. "Punctuality is irreplaceable. It cannot be bought. It cannot be transferred or used at another time," Zippy rambled on in his head. "Well, that's enough thinking for one night. I should just drive."

Stopping at another traffic light, Zippy decided to leave the main highway to shorten the driving time. He took the back roads, not frequently used.

As he made a right turn onto River Drive, he yielded to an ambulance. His thoughts quickly leaped to the poor soul or souls inside the ambulance.

"I hope they aren't DOA. Dead on Arrival is a serious way to make an entrance into a hospital," admitted Zippy to himself.

Just five minutes before, Zippy had been driving his stretch limousine like a race car. Now, after taking a final glance at the ambulance, Zippy realized that excessive speed was unwise. "You shouldn't try to compensate for the tardiness of your passengers."

The light changed to green. Instinctively, Zippy reduced his driving speed to 25 mph.

13

Missing in Action

At 8:30 p.m., Mr. Wyker stopped the music. The dancing stopped. The ballroom lights slowly brightened. Spotlights dramatically illuminated the stage. A hush fell over the crowd as Mr. Wyker finally proceeded to announce the King and Queen of the Hawthorne Hills High School Prom. Holding back their applause, everyone in the crowd swept the ballroom with their eyes like an oscillating searchlight. They wanted to catch the astonished smiles of the two winners.

"Will Mr. Ed Windsong and the lovely Ms. Turquoise Timerhorn please come to the stage to receive their crowns as King and Queen of the 2006 Hawthorne Hills High School Senior Prom?" announced the master of ceremonies, Mr. Wyker.

The prom participants exploded in boisterous applause, but no royalty advanced forward.

"I feared it might one day come to this, Turquoise!" blurted Becky, intensely spilling out her emotions in one long breath.

"What are you talking about, Becky?" Valerie inquired with a gasp.

"Turquoise's bad habit of not arriving on time will be her downfall," Becky lamented.

As if on cue, each member of the crew worried that some tragedy may have befallen the couple. Their mysterious absence seemed completely unexplainable, considering Ed's reputation for punctuality.

"Don't you guys remember the time we went to a karate flick about six months ago?" Jonathan Quincy said calmly, a martial-arts expert himself.

Irritated, Valerie responded, "Hey, man, that little Ms. Turquoise made us all wait. She finally arrived at twelve-forty in the afternoon."

"It was ten minutes after the movie had started," grumbled Griffin, "and we missed a lot of the beginning action."

All at once, the crew's collective memory clicked back into the present moment.

"Where is our favorite couple?" exclaimed Natasha.

Griffin pondered, "Turquoise is so attractive, but I wonder how Ed is dealing with her lateness tonight? Friendship is for friends, not timekeeping."

14

Why Didn't They Wait?

Zippy lowered the glass partition to deliver the good news to Mr. Windsong: "We'll be there in less than ten minutes." It was 8:45 p.m.

Without leaving any road kill against the curbs, Ed and Turquoise finally arrived in front of the Golden Paradise Hotel, *Late on Arrival*, but still alive.

Ed now put on his public face and jumped out of the car first, not waiting for Zippy to perform the customary service of opening the door for the passengers.

Ed leaned into the back seat of the car to assist his prom date to the curb. He took Turquoise's soft hand and pulled her gently out of their limo. For one brief moment, Ed looked deeply into Turquoise's eyes, in silence. No words could express his feeling at this crossroads in their relationship.

Ed guided Turquoise's elbow to escort her inside to the prom.

"No matter what has happened tonight, Edward, we can work it out."

"Let's just get inside, Ms. Timerhorn."

"Edward, why are you calling me by my last name? Call me 'Turquoise' or 'T.N.T.,' but why are you calling me 'Ms. Timerhorn,' with that tone in your voice? Don't we have the two tickets to happiness?"

Ed wore his tuxedo like it was a knight's armor and calmly allowed Turquoise's questions to go unanswered.

Ed and Turquoise were surrounded by booming applause and a roaring approval from the electrified prom crowd as they entered the ballroom.

"Edward, they love how we look," Turquoise whispered coyly into his ear. Her next statement showed even more self-confidence. "We must be the King and Queen of the Prom."

Turquoise beamed at her fellow senior classmates, oblivious to the real reasons for their excitement.

"Listen, Edward, they are chanting our names ... maybe, just maybe, they want us to go up on the stage to receive our crowns?"

"L-o-o-o-o-k," Ed projected as he pointed to the stage.

Turquoise looped her left arm around Ed's right. He led her closer to the stage. Ed first noticed a familiar 6' 10" frame on the stage. Turquoise could not miss the charming young lady to his right. Valerie was Griffin's Queen of the Prom. Ed caught Griffin's attention at the foot of the stage and congratulated both him and Valerie with a thumbs-up and a smile.

The crew joined Ed and Turquoise at the stage. They listened politely to the crew's conversation about the events that had transpired during their unfortunate absence. Ed nodded his head stoically, while Turquoise appeared dazed.

"Everyone voted for you, Ed — and Turquoise," Jonathan said in a quiet, deliberate voice.

Natasha joined in by saying, "It was almost unanimous!"

"It was the first time in Hawthorne Hills High School history that one couple got 90 percent of the votes," remarked Becky.

A moment later, Turquoise suddenly felt her skin turn prickly as a cactus. The sizzling stare of Ed's eyes landed on her. Her body temperature rose like a thermometer that had been pulled from a patient with a fever of 103 degrees.

No one needed to tell Ed what had occurred. Moments before, he had come to the full realization of what had happened this evening.

Ed put the words together for the first time. He told his date with profound disappointment, "We arrived at the prom L-A-T-E, Turquoise. The alternate royal couple on the stage won, by default.

"We were not here. Mr. Wyker couldn't crown *us!*" whispered Ed into Turquoise's ear, his chest heaving up and down slowly.

He glared deeply into Turquoise's eyes. She had never felt such apprehension before.

Ed finally continued speaking to Turquoise, "We were *late* — so they crowned two of our friends *King and Queen* of the Prom for Hawthorne Hills High School this year."

Now Ed had spelled out the consequences very succinctly. He had identified Turquoise's fatal flaw, which, previously, he had chosen to forgive.

"… But why didn't they wait?" Turquoise queried in disbelief.

"Why should they?" responded Ed. "The crowning was scheduled for 7:00 p.m. We arrived at 9:00 p.m. — two hours later. Should they have held up dinner, too?"

From the sidelines, their friends could sense their detachment whenever Ed and Turquoise danced the remaining part of the evening.

Focusing on the magic and expectation of the prom night after-party, the crew bid Ed and Turquoise goodbye as they all left the event.

Later, the silence in Ed and Turquoise's limo was broken only when Zippy, the limo driver, opened the door for the junior miss to exit. Ed had directed Zippy to stop at Chez Celeste.

"I'm very hungry, Turquoise," Ed insisted. "And I'm sure you are, too."

After a very solemn dinner, Ed paid the check with the one-hundred-dollar bill that he had always reserved for an emergency.

Downhearted in a way that was new and confusing, Turquoise had many questions and no answers. *Why do I procrastinate? What makes me lose track of time? Why do I allow my lateness to hurt my friends? Why have I forced Ed to waste his money and ruin both his and my prom?*

Ed and Turquoise reached the front door of her house a little after midnight. Turquoise forced a Hollywood smile on her face. But she thought to herself, *Why isn't Edward taking us out to meet our friends?* Then she reflected, *Perhaps he has very little money left. So maybe that's why he instructed the driver to take us directly to my address.* She put her key in the front door, remembering the day Ed had helped her father install it.

A master Native craftsman from Santa Fe, New Mexico had designed this entryway. At its center, a large, circular, frosted-glass window graced the door panel. Beige silk curtains hung over the window. A decorative letter "T" had been etched on it. The stately oak door welcomed visitors to the Timerhorns' home on Silver Saddle Road.

On this evening, Ed had become acutely aware of many things about his prom date that he had chosen to overlook. Ed had counted on her to be his potential life partner. "No one else," he had once told himself, "could make me as happy as she does. After all, Turquoise has a tremendous capacity to do whatever she wants to accomplish in life — *except to arrive on time.*"

Ed examined Turquoise's face once again. He saw that her loving eyes were moist. He saw Turquoise turn toward him and hold in her breath in expectation. She tilted her head upward, yearning to meet Edward's face, almost as if to kiss him. Ed gazed again deeply into Turquoise's dispirited, pleading eyes.

"Are you coming inside, Edward? It's still our prom night. Please. Come inside, so we can talk."

"Turquoise, it's over."

"Yes, I know that the prom is over, but can't we still spend some time together? Is it too late for me to apologize?"

"I appreciate your gesture, Turquoise, but I really feel that I must take some time to rethink our relationship."

"Edward, what has come over you? Come inside. Let's discuss this further."

"Turquoise — not now!"

Turquoise watched her "Edward" hurrying away. Having ultimately revealed his true sentiments, he got into the waiting limousine and left.

15

The Truth Be Told

Echoing thoughts of Edward's good-bye stung like an unexpected wasp bite on the ear of the uncrowned Prom Queen. *I really have hurt him terribly.* She closed the oak door with the circular window. This door held so many memories for her — of both Edward and her father. She remembered freshly how the two of them had worked together installing the customized door. It was barely two years ago that Turquoise had first introduced her new boyfriend to her father, whose hobby was woodworking. She vividly recalled how Edward had commented to her father, "Mr. Timerhorn, you have chosen such an amazing front door."

"So you like that style, eh?" Mr. Timerhorn responded as he took Ed's appreciation as a personal compliment.

As Turquoise had listened to this brief exchange, she just knew that her father's approval of Edward was his blessing on her new relationship as well.

She had thought, *Edward is the one.*

Profoundly stunned by Edward's abrupt departure, she was standing still as a corpse in the middle of the living room. Turquoise's tormented tears rained down on the polished wooden floor.

A minute passed. Turquoise thought about the last five minutes of her young seventeen-year-old life. All Turquoise could think about was Edward running away from the door and her. It was the first time he had refused to come inside — ever.

Ten more minutes passed, and Turquoise, still in her deep thoughts, unfroze and flopped down on the loveseat in the living room. The exquisite, multistranded silver necklace with precious gemstones encircling her neck suggested the sophistication and charm of a princess.

Turquoise relived the evening methodically. First, Turquoise remembered that this was the first time Edward had to spend his one-hundred-dollar bill to pay for the prom meal her lateness had caused them to miss. She knew that he never wanted to use that one-hundred-dollar bill. Turquoise remembered that Edward plainly liked having the one-hundred-dollar bill in his wallet. *Maybe, it was like a good luck charm?* Turquoise silently thought to herself, *I have been inconsiderate of Ed and very disrespectful.*

Speeding away from 505 Silver Saddle Road in the back of Zippy's limousine, it was the first time Ed had shown his now ex-girlfriend that he would no longer tolerate her disrespect, no matter how attractive she was otherwise. *Perhaps, I should have addressed this long ago,* he considered. *I may have encouraged her bad habit.*

Glancing out the dark-tinted limo window three blocks away from the Timerhorns' house, Ed became aware of feeling the dew from the Timerhorns' lawn on his shoes because he hadn't used the walkway. At the time, he'd been too preoccupied to notice. Ed hoped that the traumatic scene on the Timerhorns' front lawn just might provoke Turquoise's growth in one area — being able to be more punctual and considerate.

Back at the Timerhorns' home at 12:30 a.m., Turquoise pushed herself slowly off of what was once Ed's and her favorite seat in her home. How much she wished he was by her side. However, the once-happy surroundings of the living room no longer looked very friendly to Turquoise.

She quietly picked up her dove-white satin bag and shawl while carrying her heels in her right hand. Turquoise slid barefoot across the polished floor. As she moved slowly toward the stairs, her lifeless hair lay limply around her shoulders. Turquoise thought to herself, *I'm going upstairs to my bedroom to sleep. There is no distinction between reality and dreams while I sleep.* Something in Turquoise still wanted to repress the whole truth.

In the light of the foyer, before Turquoise got a chance to approach the staircase, she heard a warm voice pierce the night's silence.

She was frozen with emotion.

"You're home early, Turquoise. Did you have a good time?" A motherly voice embraced a child who was really a young lady.

"Sure, Mom, we had the T-I-M-E of our lives. Talk to you in the morning." Turquoise faked a big yawn to her mother so that she would not have to answer any more questions.

"Get some sleep," coaxed Teal Timerhorn as she turned off the dim lamp in the hallway. She watched her daughter drag herself, with a demeanor that oozed dejection, up the stairs to the second floor. She could barely see the top of her head over the white handrail.

Silently promising herself to understand the reason for her daughter's apparent gloom, Teal Timerhorn followed her daughter up the stairs and returned to her bedroom. She looked quietly at her husband, who was sound asleep in their bed. He was totally unaware of the turmoil Turquoise had brought upon herself. Teal removed her silk bathrobe. She eased gingerly back into the bed next to her husband, Roy.

Teal fell back asleep holding these thoughts in her mind: *I surmise, my second child, you will need to learn more about the importance of what it means to respect relationships. You must understand how to be yourself and think of what others deserve as well in order to achieve true happiness. I can only attempt to encourage positive thoughts and actions, but I can't ensure them.*

16

Can I Ever Forgive Her?

Turquoise couldn't sleep that night, and neither could Ed. She had dreams of Ed repeating the reminder, "6:00 p.m. sharp." She heard the words over and over again — "6:00 p.m. sharp, 6:00 p.m. sharp." Her usual sense of proud composure was in shambles.

Meanwhile, Ed paced the floor at his parents' home. Simultaneously, Turquoise, at 505 Silver Saddle Road, nervously tossed to and fro, from one side of her bed to the other.

A night full of promise had become one of pain, agony, and bitter regret.

Ed's persistent footsteps aroused his sleeping parents. They joined him in the living room.

"It's the end," Ed announced to his mother.

"The end of what, Ed?" responded Sabera, in a motherly tone.

"Son, nothing can be that horrible for you to lose a night's sleep," interjected Ed's father.

Ed showed his open wallet to his mother.

"Is something missing, son?"

"Mom, please listen — and you, too, Dad," Ed urged. "I had to spend the Franklin tonight — the one-hundred-dollar bill — for something totally unnecessary."

"Go ahead, son — we're listening." Ben Windsong cleared his throat as he leaned forward to capture every word.

"You know that I kept that one-hundred-dollar bill in my wallet only for an extreme emergency — but not to accommodate a fine young lady whose excessive lateness caused us to miss a fantastic dinner and forfeit our crowns. I'm having an impossible time convincing myself to forgive her."

"Sabera, honey, do you hear our phone ringing?"

"Yes, Ben, but who can that be at this hour in the morning?" Sabera whispered to her husband.

Ed walked over to the telephone and picked up the receiver.

"Hello. Hello ... who is this?"

"Who is it, son?"

"It's ... nobody," Ed replied as he hung up the telephone. "The person must have had the wrong number."

As a last-ditch effort, Turquoise had choked her words into the telephone and promised, "I'm going to change. It's my new beginning. I only hope ... Hey, wait a minute! I heard someone say hello on the other end," Turquoise blurted out loud to herself. "Was it a dropped call? Didn't I hear Edward's voice?"

Across town, tears streamed down the pitiful face of a girl who up until now, had everything a high school senior could possibly want.

17

We're in This Dilemma Together

The silvery light of dawn hadn't appeared on the horizon yet, as Teal Timerhorn dialed Sabera Windsong on the telephone. Teal, a marathon runner who had crossed the finish line in Central Park five consecutive years, knew how to be a winner.

As the busy Director of Human Resources for a Fortune 500 company, Teal was known to her colleagues as a tough but fair manager. She was always able to elicit the best performance from her staff as well as plot the next career move for her company's rising stars.

On several occasions, she had admitted to her running partner Donna, "It seems easier to handle my hectic workload than to deal with the formidable task of supporting and advising my teenage daughter into responsible adulthood."

Teal needed to talk it out. Breathing in deeply and exhaling to energize her 5' 3", 105-pound frame, her assertive voice blared into Mrs. Windsong's speakerphone.

"Good morning, Sabera. I know you must be wondering why I am including you on my AM calling list." Teal paused before going on. "But my Turquoise *is not* 'Turquoise'. She's downright midnight blue."

Sabera cut her friend's speech off abruptly and replied, "Say no more, Teal. We also have realized that the prom night was a real nightmare for our two children."

"A nightmare?"

"Yes. It was a disastrous prom, the way my son related it to Ben and me. Why would Ed come home as early as 1:00 a.m. on prom night if he was really having a great time with Turquoise?"

"H-m-m-m."

"He told us he would be home after sunrise. Do you get my drift? Let me put it to you this way, Teal: Why would Ed show me an open wallet with money in it and complain only about the missing one-hundred-dollar bill?"

Hesitant to say a word, Teal said, in an unusually reticent tone, "Please go on."

Sabera paused a second and then went on to explain, "Ed just kept on repeating, when he arrived home, '6 o'clock sharp … had to use my … one-hundred-dollar Franklin tonight.' Ed missed out tonight and felt absolutely distraught, because they arrived late at the prom. He and Turquoise not only missed the prom dinner but also forfeited their crowns to the alternates."

Gazing at the rays on the early June horizon, Sabera tilted her venetian blinds. It allowed all the golden morning sunlight to flood into her immaculate kitchen. A five-inch, black musical clef note, along with other notes, were painted on one orange wall as a mural.

Sabera waited now for a response from her dear friend.

Sitting in her kitchen, kept clean by her two daughters, Rita and Turquoise, Teal attempted to gather her thoughts and gave Sabera her best shot by uttering, "Knowing your son, Sabera, '6 o'clock sharp' meant just that." Teal's voice trailed off softly in an uncommon whisper, recalling how late Turquoise had been on the prior evening.

Realizing she had the upper hand in the conversation, Sabera spoke directly: "Why can't Turquoise be on time?"

Teal heard the hurtful and agonizing indictment spoken by Sabera. Teal could no longer ignore the facts. Every word was the truth. Recovering her stellar skills as a smooth negotiator, Teal deftly shifted the topic away from Turquoise's tardiness to a different note.

She asked Sabera about her family: "Does your cousin Eva still live in Many Farms, Arizona?"

"To be exact, she lives in both places. She lives both in Many Farms and also in Santa Fe, New Mexico," informed Sabera. She added, "By the way, Teal, Eva is a talented counselor."

Motherhood was a common thread between the two women, and they often shared their feelings on this subject with each other.

"What am I going to do with Turquoise?" Teal said meekly to her friend for the first time. Teal was baffled by Turquoise's lack of consideration for others.

Knowing that Teal was terribly troubled by Turquoise's lateness, Sabera consoled, "If you want to talk further, you know that I will help you in any way I can."

Teal anxiously glanced at her watch. She then abruptly said, "I've got to go … it's 5:44 a.m. I want to run at least five miles before I go into the office this morning. We'll chat again, Sabera. Thanks so much for listening."

"Any time, Teal — we're in this dilemma together."

Sabera hung up the telephone. She recognized, *Yes, as parents we are in this dilemma together. However, I feel that Turquoise has the more challenging road ahead.*

She briskly started her morning routine of composing music. As a renowned performer of cultural narratives, she had a large following among New Yorkers who were interested in the first inhabitants of the Americas.

18

Moving On

At 5:00 a.m. every morning, Ed would diligently rise and take care of the gardens in the front and back yards for his mother. Along with carpentry and basketball, this was one of his favorite leisure activities. There was something so satisfying about working in nature. This morning, the sky looked spectacular. The clarity of the blue was punctuated by gentle sweeps of white wispy clouds.

After the events of the last few weeks, it was good to be able to relax with his thoughts. Ed recollected, *the toughest thing to do is to end a relationship gracefully and with as little rancor as possible.*

Just then a tall willowy figure dressed in coveralls dashed by. It was Ed's neighbor, Stephanie Strong. They had attended the same parochial high school until Ed switched to Hawthorne Hills. Ed and Stephanie had worked on the scenery for the freshman and sophomore year-end musical productions. Both knew their way around a two-by-four and an electric saw. Stephanie had learned the trade by volunteering for "Donated Dwellings." With five home projects under her belt, she was now assisting the foreman with managing the other volunteers.

Ed had always admired her vivacious style. Anything Stephanie put her mind to, she accomplished. Yes, she seemed a bit *too* focused, perhaps, but he respected her determination and commitment to public service. Stephanie had also cultivated the necessity to get things done in a timely fashion.

Impulsively, Ed shouted out, "Hey, neighbor!", hoping to catch her attention. Stephanie whirled around briefly and acknowledged the greeting by playfully remarking, "Do I know you?" She slowed her pace long enough to add, "Congratulations to us on our graduations!" And, with that, Stephanie picked up her tempo so that she could make the 5:17 a.m. Q train, musing to herself ... *the one that got away!*

Ed contemplated to himself, *I'm going to ask her if she would take me on a tour of her current affordable-housing project. It will give me a chance to reconnect with her.*

19

Graduation

It had now been three weeks and three days since the prom. By chance, Turquoise got another opportunity to sit next to "her Edward," at the Hawthorne Hills High School graduation, held on the Promenade Level of the Golden Paradise Hotel.

It took the strong-arm effort of her two siblings and two parents to marshal Turquoise to her own graduation — thirty minutes early. The violet tassel on the graduation mortarboard had a ten-carat gold charm dangling off the side.

Turquoise closed her eyes briefly.

"Isn't this where the prom was held three weeks ago, Turquoise?" asked Mr. Timerhorn. Hearing her father's voice, she automatically opened her eyes and lamented, "Yes, Dad .... This was the very scene of the fiasco."

Teal Timerhorn removed a camera from her purse. Waving it back and forth, she cheerfully said to Turquoise, "Let's take a picture here."

"Mom-m-m, do we have to? Let's go inside. I don't want to be late," quipped Turquoise. "It's already 8:55 a.m."

The Timerhorn family was shocked at Turquoise's request.

"Yes, darling, you're right. Let's go inside."

"We'll have plenty of *time* to take pictures inside. It's your day, Turquoise," Roy proudly agreed with his second-born child.

While they faced the elevators, a new "family joke" developed: *Turquoise wanted to be on time.*

The elevator arrived and lifted them to the Promenade Level. All family members heard shouts of congratulations to the graduates. The Timerhorns mingled into the sea of joyous acclaim of parents for their children.

Ushers tried desperately to separate relatives from the graduates. One usher recognized her statuesque beauty and suggested Turquoise proceed directly to the stage. She ascended the stairs and gracefully took her assigned seat.

Turquoise sat in the front row, the first seat. Next to her, she noticed the placard with *"Reserved — E. Windsong"* written on it. No sooner did Turquoise turn her head than her former Mr. Wonderful appeared — "her Edward."

Ed first greeted the three other students on stage and took his place next to Turquoise. His very presence there made her heart pulsate faster.

M-m-m, this may be a second chance, Turquoise thought to herself as she turned to face Ed. She leaned over and softly uttered into Ed's ear, using her most polite, honeysuckle-like voice,

"Hello, Edward. I haven't heard from you since ..."

"Please, Turquoise," Ed whispered back firmly into Turquoise's ear. A second later, he forced a polite grin on his chiseled face and shook his head "No."

Turquoise's heart plummeted. She masked her disappointment by putting on her trademark smile, now a mere accessory to her graduation gown.

While waiting, each of these graduates spent their time reflecting on their former relationships. Ed recalled how lucky he felt the day he and Turquoise had met after a basketball game that first fall at Hawthorne Hills High School.

Enthralled with his athletic talent, Turquoise had taken the lead and congratulated Ed after a winning game.

Ed confidently invited Turquoise to a nearby coffee shop, where they continued their conversation for a couple of hours. He immediately felt at ease with her. They shared a common interest in possibly pursuing a business career, although Ed had been considering law as well. Everything seemed to go so well. Even their mothers got to know each other through school activities and really hit it off. Ed had come to deeply appreciate Roy Timerhorn's sense of style and design as he worked with him while making improvements to the Timerhorn home.

It seemed that nothing could disrupt the good times he spent with Turquoise and the crew. What could be more wonderful than the times he and Turquoise had spent whole afternoons luxuriating in different parks and museums in New York City?

But then Turquoise's lack of punctuality had become an increasing obstacle in their blossoming relationship. It seemed that no activity that they shared failed to begin without Turquoise being late. How embarrassed Ed had felt when, time after time, Turquoise had been late for a movie or an outing with the crew! At last, the prom had made a happy future together seem impossible.

Meanwhile, Turquoise could not bring herself to understand why their excited anticipation of college was not able to outweigh the importance of this single debacle. *If only we had been able to arrive a half-hour early, we would have been crowned King and Queen.*

The 9:30 a.m. graduation ceremony began promptly.

The principal of Hawthorne Hills High School, Ms. Vivian Tuftmarks, first congratulated all the graduates.

During the middle of the graduation ceremony, Ms. Tuftmarks signaled with her left hand for five of the graduates on the stage to rise. Principal Tuftmarks announced Hawthorne Hills's Student Achievement Awards. She paused a moment and stated regally, "Ms. Turquoise Nez Timerhorn has the highest average in the senior class of 378 students. She is our Valedictorian."

A thunderous applause began as Turquoise strode daintily to the center stage in order to accept this prestigious academic award.

Ms. Tuftmarks warmly shook Turquoise's right hand while presenting her with the plaque using the other hand. Not letting her hand go, Ms. Tuftmarks eased Turquoise closer to her in full view of the audience. She whispered a mysterious message into Turquoise's ear before letting their handshake go. After hearing about the fact that she and Ed had to forfeit the King and Queen crowns at the prom, Ms. Tuftmarks wanted to take a final opportunity to advise Turquoise.

Teal Timerhorn noticed the unusual gesture on the stage. She nudged her husband and inquired, "What do you think the principal is saying to our daughter, Roy?"

Mr. Timerhorn, a man of wit and wisdom, turned his head and smiled at his puzzled wife. "Teal, I'll tell you the very next time I wear a tuxedo," joked Roy Timerhorn to his wife. He was sure he knew the answer already.

Next, Principal Tuftmarks asked the school band to play Hawthorne Hills High School's rally song. Then, Ms. Tuftmarks announced proudly, "Mr. Ed Windsong, Captain of the Cranes Basketball Team, whose unbeatable record of having the most victories in the last two years has made us all proud to be from Hawthorne Hills High School."

Ms. Tuftmarks paused to allow the rousing applause to subside and then trumpeted Ed's two other outstanding accomplishments into the microphone.

Continuing in an imperial voice, Ms. Tuftmarks said, "In addition, Ed 'The Scholarman' Windsong had time to maintain the second-highest scholastic average. Ed is our Salutatorian," she concluded.

Besides being principal, Ms. Vivian Elizabeth Tuftmarks also taught an English Regents class. She was a master teacher as well as a superior administrator. Principal Tuftmarks gave each student her most challenging and often grueling reading assignments, homework on Fridays, and tough grades as well.

With grace and poise, Ms. Tuftmarks finished presenting the awards to the top students. Turquoise held onto her own chair. She tried to decipher Ms. Tuftmarks' unexpected graduation message.

Walking down the stage steps, on their way down to join the recessional, Turquoise turned her head back toward Ed to catch his attention hoping he would give her an opportunity to apologize again for the prom disaster. Fortune did not shine on her that day. The other honorees formed a wall between them as they descended. Giving up, she continued down the stairs.

Turquoise rejoined her family, and they left immediately to continue the graduation celebration at home. Meanwhile, Ed's family, joined by the Strong and Harris families, proceeded to celebrate at the Overlook Restaurant.

THE JOURNEY
CONTINUES
(PART II)

20

Out with the Tide

One week later, reveling in the call of freedom, the newly graduated crew members set out for a July party at Jones Beach on Long Island, New York. In contrast to their glamorous limousine rides to the prom, they took the Long Island Railroad to this big shindig. The 9:04 a.m. train pulled into Jamaica station. The group was there on time. They sat together in the same section.

A bit restless, Griffin Lee Browne still gloated inwardly about his and Valerie's winning the prom crowns. He rose from his seat to provoke some fun before arriving at the beach. As he swaggered down the aisle as if he were the conductor collecting tickets, he confronted each individual with the same question, "Whose bright idea was this, anyway?"

Natasha Orlov answered Griffin's sarcastic question with the soothing words, "It's a comfortable ride to Jones Beach — besides, you can enjoy the scenery."

"I agree with you, Tasha," said the newcomer to the crew. "My view is wonderful," Stephanie Strong stated as she tossed her auburn hair to look directly at Ed with a mischievous smile.

Sensing Stephanie's *double entendre*, Becky Córpuz defended the memory of her classy best friend, Turquoise.

Stephanie Strong is definitely wrong for ... Becky thought to herself. But that was a conversation for later.

For the most part, the crew deeply regretted Ed and Turquoise's breakup in spite of its inevitability.

Nevertheless, Griffin told Ed, "Your new girl is a perfect match for you." Griffin uttered this loud enough for everyone to hear.

However, Ed only slightly nodded his head and made no comment.

"You must admit, Becky, that we were all on time today," acknowledged Natasha.

Jonathan, with his sharp wit and dry humor, piped in and said, "Maybe, but you shouldn't trade a lady in for a timepiece."

Ed tried to ignore the remarks made by some of his closest friends. He closed his eyes for a moment. He understood the implications, which left him with doubt and then irritation.

Ed had barely broken up with Turquoise when his interest in Stephanie had taken them both by surprise. Now Stephanie had to conclude that Ed seemed to be on the rebound.

Meanwhile, Griffin unconsciously revealed a secret affection. He still harbored a crush on the girl with the solar-power smile. He thoughtlessly complimented her by saying to his pal Ed, "Turquoise is a hard act to follow ... for us all."

"Spare me!" asserted Valerie. She had begun to feel taken for granted. Having shown her care, not only for Griffin, but also for his widower father, she helped around the house, especially with cooking. She often felt her efforts were not appreciated for the sincere affection they were intended to be.

"Speaking of Turquoise," asked Jonathan, "what is she doing these days?"

"She is a working lady now. After graduation, Turquoise got a job at a medicine place," Colón enlightened the group.

"Oh, Colón, my love, you mean a pharmaceutical company." Rebecca told her companion. She was displaying her top-notch vocabulary.

"You know what I mean," insisted Colón to Becky.

"By the way, talking of summer jobs, where are you applying, Ed?" Jonathan Quincy asked.

"I'm still considering an internship with my current company, Bracy, Wong & Lopez, but Turquoise also encouraged me months ago to apply to the same company that accepted her. So, I'll see which position might work out the best this summer."

"Any way; anyhow; any who! Let's enjoy the freedom we have. It's July, and school is out. In two months, we'll all be in college and working harder than ever," declared Valerie.

During the six hours on the beach, unexpected things transpired. Stephanie nibbled up much of Ed's lunch. "Ed won't mind," Stephanie told herself. "We can buy some burgers and hot dogs later."

Ed had assumed Stephanie would bring her own lunch. With all her talents, social amenities, like preparing a picnic lunch for Ed and her, had not been on her radar.

"Ed," she apologized, "I'm so sorry I didn't think to bring snacks or a lunch for today. It just didn't occur to me, and I feel terribly embarrassed. I'm so used to grabbing a quick sandwich and beverage on the job."

Stephanie added in a hush, "I feel I must be completely honest with you. I'm so grateful for our friendship. My social life has pretty much been limited to hanging out after hours with my coworkers."

Endeared by her sincerity, Ed responded, "Stephanie, thanks for reorganizing your work schedule so you could join me today. Don't take the food issue too seriously and — for that matter — some of the conversation that you've heard. I understand. Neither of us has a diploma in maturity yet. And yes, we all appreciate the fact that everyone was punctual today."

As Griffin enjoyed his girlfriend's suntan lotion massage, he drifted off into a light slumber. *I had Turquoise's attention all to myself my whole sophomore year in biology. Next, Ed 'The Scholarman' Windsong showed up at Hawthorne Hills High in our junior year. Then, Ed met our lovely Ms. Timerhorn, the girl with beauty and brains.* He remembered her magical words that made his knees buckle — "Griffin, my muffin."

Griffin asked himself, *Why haven't I gotten over Turquoise's flattery? After all, I have never had a date with her. Infatuation is pure fantasy, and I feel trapped by it.*

The undeniable fact was that Ed and Turquoise had been inseparable from the beginning of their junior year in high school. That is, until now.

21

Ominously Late

The once-pleasant face of Turquoise Nez Timerhorn changed instantly as an earthquake of discovery was certainly about to happen. Nowhere to run, nowhere to hide.

Turquoise's long, slender fingers beat against the elevator button frantically.

Overtaken by her desperation, she started to pace in front of the lobby's elevator door.

Here they come. How can I avoid them? sighed Turquoise to herself in a silent prayer. She pulled back her shoulders and cranked her head to the right. She saw her escape route.

"The stairs," Turquoise whispered. With soundless steps, she crept toward the stairs.

"O-O-oh no. I'm trapped! This exit door will sound an alarm if I open it," exclaimed Turquoise as she read the sign on the door. She scurried from side to side, like a rabbit escaping a predator.

Turquoise was working as a summer intern at a pharmaceutical company. It had been exactly seven weeks since that fateful day of her senior prom. In the lobby of her office building, Turquoise used her keen eyesight to focus on the fast-approaching entourage of dignitaries.

There could be no mistake. She moaned softly so that only she could hear the tremble in her voice, "I'm caught. Here they come. Not only do I see my boss, but also his boss and the CEO, too."

Sucking in her breath, Turquoise asked herself, *Did they see me? If I ever have been in the wrong place at the wrong time, then this has to be it.*

Feeling her knees weaken, she tried to hide her face behind a Southwestern art magazine she had just purchased. Reporting her own death to the jewelry ad on page twenty-four, she sadly closed her eyelids, confessing silently, *I'm dead. They have caught me again for being ...*

Startled at the noise of a motor, Turquoise turned her body around to witness the unhoped-for.

She heard the comforting noise of the steel elevator doors slowly opening. She was twenty feet from being discovered before her escape arrived. She was rescued by a swift step and a sigh into the upward-bound elevator. The concealing doors closed behind her. Turquoise pressed the button for her work floor.

The elevator sped up toward the forty-fourth floor. Turquoise pondered her predicament. *This isn't cool. Being on time rules! There's got to be a better way to live,* she chided herself.

Feeling confident — since no one could witness this confession on an empty elevator — Turquoise shared her thoughts out loud with the four small walls around her. "What would I have said to them? I would have been caught without an alibi for being late to work today."

Turquoise smoothed down her thick, raven hair. It sparkled under the intense fluorescent lights. Exiting the elevator with more composure and a slower heartbeat, Turquoise strolled boldly to her desk. She looked at the pile of papers in her inbox. She cheerfully switched into her top-performance work mode. How she wished that her talents and gifts would not have to be employed as a cover for her less-than-stellar qualities. Her academics and work ethic were impeccable. Yet, it seemed that all of this was eclipsed by her lack of punctuality. She regretted, once again, her mismanagement of time on the day of the prom.

The next day, as Turquoise sorted reports, she stumbled upon an unread memorandum sent to her. It was an internal memo with her name on it. She read it anxiously. Her heart started to flutter.

The memo was a notice to her that she had a morning meeting about a week later. She closed her eyes briefly, trying to picture in her mind what this important meeting might be about.

Turquoise thought to herself, *It's not every day that you meet with the CEO of a company along with the Human Resource Deputy Director.*

Scratching her head, she lacked any rational idea at this point as to why she had received this request.

I wonder what this meeting will be about, Turquoise interrogated herself like a detective. *I'd better write this down in my daily planner.*

She reached for a red pen and scribbled in her organizer. Turquoise wrote, *9:00 a.m. on the 24th of July at Ms. London's office. It's on the 6th floor, the Human Resources Department of Best Pharmaceutical Company.* Without warning, an alarm suddenly went off in her head.

Her unwise use of her time had caught up with her. She asked herself, *Has my continual tardiness become a problem? Did the delay of twenty-five minutes make a difference in my sterling performance yesterday?* She continued to think, *I just had to have my manicure that morning so that my nails could match my dress.*

Then, Turquoise brushed aside any negative thoughts. After all, she'd planned to work two hours overtime today to "make up" for her lost time yesterday.

At the end of the afternoon, she pulled her hair back into a ponytail. It was the end of a long day, including two extra hours of "self-imposed" payless overtime.

She vowed to be *on time,* forever, starting tomorrow.

Tomorrow came, and she was on time. But then she was late the very next day after her "*forever tomorrow.*"

Just in Time

On a blistering July 19th, temperatures had been rising before daylight hours. Showgirl legs hit the sidewalk at 9:02 a.m., moving swifter than a cheetah pursued by hunters. It was Turquoise, dashing from her taxi on that Wednesday morning, headed for her 9-to-5 summer job.

She rushed into work with a briefcase slung over her right shoulder. She closed her wallet, which was now depleted by the $10.50 ride. This was the price she paid for the adrenaline-pumping, time-racing, car-whizzing ride in an attempt to recapture lost time. Turquoise was the great manipulator of time, or so she thought.

She confidently walked into the crowded lobby of her summer employer, Best Pharmaceutical Company. With her head held high and an invincible look in her eyes, Turquoise checked her watch while she waited for the elevator to arrive.

It was 9:06 a.m. *No more taking a taxi to work. Besides, it's too expensive, and I'm still late,* contemplated Turquoise as she absentmindedly filed into a packed, air-conditioned elevator.

A broken promise is not redeemable even if you've made it to yourself. Turquoise lowered her head to avoid anyone's gaze. Encaged, she was lifted up to the forty-fourth floor.

Passing the fortieth floor, the elevator slowed down to the next express stop, the forty-fourth floor. The doors opened. Turquoise's razor-sharp eyes alerted her to someone sitting at her desk. She stepped off the elevator and moved boldly toward her workstation — "her territory."

A cheerful masculine voice greeted her with striking green eyes. "Oh, good morning, Ms. Timerhorn," the intruder spoke up. This fair-haired man was occupying Turquoise's chair.

Who is this broad-shouldered gentleman firmly tapping on my neatly organized desk?

In his right hand, she noticed the company's familiar pen. Its inscription read,

"Time is a precious commodity.
If you lose it, it's lost forever."

The clock on the wall chimed 9:15 a.m. Gasping for air, Turquoise looked at the portrait of the CEO of her company that hung adjacent to her desk on the wall next to the clock. She then stammered, "G-G-Good morning, M – M – M … Mr. Best."

Calmly, the Chief Executive Officer of one of the largest pharmaceutical companies in the world asked politely, "Did you receive my memo for our meeting on the twenty-fourth?"

Turquoise lifted the memo off the top tray of her organized desk to show him. Thoroughly chagrined, she was mute.

Mr. Karl Stephan Best, not waiting for a reply from a speechless employee, stood up. "See you next week." Glancing at the clock, he added, "Our appointment is at 9:00 a.m. on July 24th. That's next Monday."

Mr. Best's words hit her like a herd of shoppers trying to grab up sales at a department store. He turned abruptly and left the forty-fourth-floor office, with Turquoise standing dazed in her thoughts.

At noon, Turquoise took her lunch break early. Stepping onto the sizzling-hot Manhattan sidewalks, she overheard two runners complain about the near-ninety-degree heat.

On this Wednesday, she decided to take only a thirty-minute lunch break instead of her normal, relaxing one hour. She started to return to the office after twenty minutes with a slight stomachache. The unannounced appearance of Mr. Best had left her with an eerie feeling.

Preoccupied with her thoughts of how to improve her work situation, Turquoise murmured, "Maybe I can score points in other areas."

A worried Turquoise crossed the street absentmindedly.

A dusty, old, blue-and-gray Mack truck with Pennsylvania license plates came barreling down the avenue. The driver of this vehicle had been on the road for ten hours straight to meet a delivery deadline just five minutes away.

A mysterious strong arm snatched Turquoise out of harm's way. The Mack truck narrowly missed hitting her. It stopped barely six inches away from Turquoise, who had slipped onto the rough pavement.

Fluttering her eyelashes in utter shock, Turquoise opened her eyes seconds later to discover a circle of strangers huddled around her and staring. Shoeless and speechless, Turquoise was helped to rise from what might have turned into a chalk drawing outline on Lexington Avenue.

"Boy, you're lucky to be alive, Miss," one male voice said. "If it wasn't for that brave young man ..."

"Yeah, who would have thought that he could run so fast?" a female voice continued, "And to be able to pull you out of the way so swiftly."

"His quick reflexes were amazing," murmured another spectator.

In all the confusion, Turquoise noticed that her wristwatch was missing. She brushed off the soot from her two-piece, navy-blue suit.

"What happened to my watch?" asked Turquoise. She smiled gratefully at the onlookers and asked for assistance. Thirty-seven lunch-time-hour volunteers joined in the hunt for Turquoise's lost D. Blackfoot & Company watch.

The search held up the hectic traffic for more than twenty minutes, with constant honking. Realizing that she had only ten minutes left of her one-hour lunch break, Turquoise thanked her army of volunteers by giving each helper her personal electrifying smile and sincere expressions of gratitude.

She abandoned her apparently lost watch but not the pursuit of the mystery man who'd risked his life to save hers. She hobbled back to her office shaken and disheveled, and slightly dirty.

Who might he have been? Turquoise asked herself each time as she repeated the miraculous story to her coworkers of how she was saved by someone still unidentified.

I will continue to tell my incredible story to all of my friends, pondered Turquoise later. *That gentleman will be my hero forever! This wonderful man knows how to take command in a high-risk situation. The crew will never believe this extraordinary rescue.*

Turquoise dialed Becky's telephone line at her job. She was out of the office, and Turquoise chose not to leave a detailed message. Next, she dialed the rest of the crew's telephone numbers and left voice messages on their telephones.

The message was the same for all. "I want to personally meet and thank a man of this caliber who would risk his life to save mine — a life unknown to him."

Away from the glitz of the Manhattan skyline, the unidentified hero recalled the crush of onlookers who had crowded around Turquoise. He had chosen to slip away. He didn't wait for any thanks. But, before he made his exit, he retrieved something priceless from the ground.

Arriving home in Brooklyn from Manhattan, Turquoise's hero removed a stunning wristwatch from his pocket.

He scanned his bedroom and noticed a flashing red signal on his answering machine, indicating a voice message was waiting. He pressed the button to retrieve the message and listened carefully to a familiar voice. The unanticipated message in Turquoise's voice on his answering machine brought a sigh of relief. She was safely out of harm's way. Griffin Lee Browne, the man of the hour, reflected on his heroic feat. How lucky he was to have been in the neighborhood making a delivery for the "Feed the Seniors" food pantry. He was on his way back to his vehicle when he intervened in the emergency rescue. He had always felt shy about his crush on Turquoise, and he told himself impulsively, *I couldn't bring myself to reveal my identity in that overwhelming setting. Returning the watch will give me a perfect opportunity later.*

23

Life Is Good

Sabera Windsong couldn't push another note onto the music sheet that she was composing and decided to take a break. She stood up, walked out of the den, and headed to the kitchen. Without pressing the speed button on the telephone, she dialed the number of a person she knew would always answer at 5:00 a.m.

"Hi, Teal," Sabera whispered softly into the phone this Tuesday morning. She looked out the window in her kitchen at the darkness of the sky just before daybreak.

"Well, hello there, Sabera — what's on your mind?" pondered Teal Timerhorn, since Sabera was not an early riser like herself.

"Oh, I wanted to remind you about us getting together on Tuesday," said Sabera, to confirm.

"Yes, I see that I wrote our appointment down in my daily planner book for July 25th — Tuesday. That's two days away," agreed Teal Timerhorn.

Fully dressed in navy-blue shorts and a white, short-sleeve t-shirt, Teal was preparing for her predawn departure to run her usual five miles.

Before Teal hung up the portable kitchen telephone, she asked her neighbor a rhetorical question, "What earth-shattering event could stop us, Sabera, from going shopping for our autumn wardrobes?"

"Yeah — you're right. Pick you up at four o'clock on Tuesday," said Sabera. She hung up the phone.

Through her musical talents and training, Sabera sensed an imbalance in the atmosphere. Without warning, a familiar voice interrupted her thoughts: "Good morning, mother — why are you up so early today?" asked Ed.

"Did I wake you, son?" Sabera asked in a voice no louder than the breeze floating through a wheat field. She took steps back and forth near the stove in her bright kitchen.

"Would you like a hot cup of herbal tea?" asked Sabera. This time, there were two strong male voices answering her in the affirmative — her loving husband Ben and their only child, Ed. The Windsong family shared the early morning meal together.

"Life is good," commented Ben. "Life could be simple, even in an overcrowded town like New York City, where so many people live never seeing the sky filled with stars. However, no skyscrapers can compare with the natural wonders the

Creator has given to mankind, like the Grand Canyon, with its awe-inspiring rock formations."

"What a wonderful place for a vacation spot," concluded Sabera.

Ed then reminded his parents, "I start my summer internship at Best Pharmaceutical tomorrow. I'm interning in the Contracts area of the Legal Department on the twenty-fifth floor. I think I'm going to enjoy learning how contracts are negotiated. I'm grateful to Turquoise for this job lead, but I need to give us a lot more time to adjust before I try to reconnect with her."

A Pink Slip

After Mr. Best's visit last Wednesday, on July 19th, life was not comfortable for Turquoise, the Hawthorne Hills graduate who had top honors. It was Monday morning, July 24th. Ms. London glanced at the huge glass mirror clock on the wall of the Human Resources Department.

She recalled that it had been about four years since the workmen had struggled to hang the clock on the wall. She had worked for Mr. Best for fifteen years, always arriving twenty to thirty minutes early for work and enjoying every minute of it. Mr. Best was a man she had grown to admire.

Ms. London, an executive assistant, shifted her attention back to the present. As she slipped an employee's file from her cabinet, she quipped, "The workmen's struggle was easier than what I have to do today."

The door swung open. "Good morning, Mr. Best," said Ms. London as she looked up from her papers with her usual welcoming smile.

Lorraine London saw her boss's eyes darting around her office as if he had lost something. She sensed his focused instinct to keep on the trail until its completion. Before he even spoke, she anticipated her boss's question.

Ms. London diplomatically stated with pursed lips, "She hasn't arrived yet."

Grumbling back, Mr. Best torpedoed a remark to his well-trained executive assistant, "Well, when she does, please accompany her to the conference room," instructed Mr. Best. "I'll be waiting there." The CEO of Best Pharmaceutical Company, a multibillion-dollar business, afforded opportunities for Business Management interns who arrived on time.

Mr. Best, statuesque at 6' 2", with business matters on his mind, had to take time out of a hectic schedule to intervene in this HR pilot program. As he waited, he pondered, *when things get out of hand, one must step in.*

During a routine security meeting a week ago, a competent manager had made an astute observation on the elevators' wide-angle camera tapes used for identifying unwanted intruders.

As the time and date were flashed across the screen, Mr. Best put together a profile of an employee who consistently entered the building after 9:00 a.m.

"An employee is caught, along with her famous elevator confession," mused Mr. Best. He heard Turquoise reveal her secret to the elevator walls. It had been captured on videotape on July 17th.

"What would I have said to them? I would have been caught without an alibi for being late to work today," Turquoise's voice was heard to say on the tape.

Mr. Best recalled his reaction that fateful Monday afternoon after he viewed all the tapes for that day.

Mr. Best was aghast at the lawless liberty under which this new employee operated. He had immediately ordered a memo to be sent to Ms. Timerhorn. Twenty-one minutes later, Ms. London brought him the memo to initial it. He tried to soften the severity of the matter. He joked sarcastically to Ms. London and said, "Bring this memo directly to our *'Employee of the Month,'* Ms. Timerhorn — exactly on July 18th at 8:30 a.m."

Scrupulously covering all bases, Ms. London asked her boss, "Wouldn't it be quicker to send her an e-mail message, sir?"

"No. I want her to have this memo in hard copy to hang on to," scolded Mr. Best. He scribbled his initials on the memo — "K.S.B." — and added gruffly, "Please, take her this memo."

Mr. Best ended the evening of July 17th pondering about this troubled employee, whom he believed had great potential. She was so much like his own daughter, except for the punctuality problem.

For Turquoise, the hands of time finally stopped on Monday, July 24th at 9:00 a.m.

Turquoise was reporting to the sixth floor instead of to her desk on the forty-fourth floor. She was breathing a little bit faster than usual. Turquoise swallowed a lump in her throat and counted backward from fifteen to zero.

Taking fifteen steps to land right in front of Suite 609, Ms. London's office, Turquoise counted aloud, "4 … 3 … 2 … 1 …," reassuring herself that this couldn't be the end of her journey.

She strolled softly onto the plush carpet inside the executive suite. Turquoise entered the room sheepishly at 9:10 a.m.

"Good morning, Ms. London," Turquoise said smoothly as she peered directly into the cold steel-blue eyes of the Human Resources Director.

"Ms. Timerhorn, please go directly into the conference room on your left. Mr. Best is waiting for you."

A quick glance at the clock on the office wall gave Turquoise the reality check of her life. Quietly murmuring to herself, "I'm already ten minutes late for my nine o'clock appointment. But, it's really not my fault that I missed a train and had to take the next one."

Assuming Turquoise's sudden pause indicated some confusion, Ms. London motioned with her left hand and pointed with her finger in the direction of the conference room. She said to Turquoise, "Please wait, and go with me."

Turquoise walked into the conference room hesitantly. She sat down at the highly polished cherry-wood conference table across from Mr. Best. Ms. London stoically followed her into the Executive Chamber.

The eyes had it. Turquoise's hazel eyes surveyed the elegant conference room and met a pair of light-green eyes.

"Good morning, Ms. *T-i-m-e*-r-h-o-r-n." Mr. Best greeted Turquoise with a chilly stare.

Turquoise would forever remember the expression on Mr. Best's face. A glance at her new watch told Turquoise the whole agenda of this meeting.

At the end of the meeting, Mr. Best suggested, in a fatherly tone, "Once you have completed college, please consider returning for an interview with my company again. Your college experience will afford you an opportunity for greater maturity."

Holding back her tears, Turquoise respectfully responded with a humble "Thank you" to Mr. Best and left the premises of her former employer.

Change in Plans

It was July 25th and, after a steady diet of shopping and bargain hunting, the two friends, Sabera and Teal, rested their tired feet. They were dining and chatting at their favorite restaurant. They had eaten there every month for the past two years, ever since their children had met and started dating each other in high school. Ed and Turquoise had hit it off from the start, studying together for exams, working in student government, and, of course, their shared interests in several other school activities. They seemed inseparable, especially to their friends.

Their monthly routine of having a sumptuous salmon dinner with crunchy fresh vegetables made these friends memorable customers at the International Seafood Cove.

"Ladies, may I get you your usual?" inquired Peter, the prompt waiter. Remembering his regular clients' favorite drinks made his customers good tippers. Peter stood at attention to confirm their beverage orders once again.

"Mrs. Windsong, that would be a peppermint tea for you, and, Mrs. Timerhorn — for you — half a glass of orange juice with grapefruit juice," Peter recalled with pride Mrs. Timerhorn's signature drink.

"Please give me a shot of bourbon, neat," demanded Teal. "Make sure there's no ice in my drink," insisted Mrs. Timerhorn in an agitated-toned voice.

Sabera took off her straw hat in consternation and put it on the red tablecloth. She and the waiter peered into the troubled visage of her best friend who had just ordered such a strong drink. Peter walked away briskly to fulfill their requests.

When they were alone again, Sabera leaned forward. She wanted to find out what was bothering Teal.

"Did you have a rough day at the office, Teal?" Sabera asked as she tried to decipher Teal's facial expressions. She knew that working outside the home could be stressful at times.

"I remember when you were a homemaker like myself. You told me that you enjoyed staying home and taking care of your three children and husband," Sabera summarized.

"No, it's not my job. It's Turquoise."

"I'm listening."

"Yesterday, Turquoise was fired from her summer job."

"For what reason was she fired, Teal? She graduated just last month with the highest average from Hawthorne Hills High School. Besides, she's great in Chemistry, so says my son Ed," rambled Sabera.

"Yes, Turquoise is all those things." Teal's voice broke as her lower lip quivered.

Peter, the waiter, returned with the peppermint tea and the shot of bourbon, as requested. He quickly put down the two drinks on the table. He then overheard the intense conversation and did the respectful thing by retreating without asking for the dinner order.

"How is Turquoise taking her dismissal?" This was Sabera's gentle way of telling Teal that she had more than a little personal knowledge of Turquoise, the young lady whom her son used to date.

As Sabera continued to quiz her shopping partner, Teal listened, motionless. The glass of bourbon remained on the table in front of her — untouched.

After seven minutes, she slowly withdrew her fingers from around the glass. Teal centered herself.

She moved beyond her own doubt and anger. Reason ruled again. Astonished at herself for resorting to liquor to fix a problem, Teal Timerhorn beckoned the waiter back to the table with a turn of her wrist.

Peter appeared promptly with her tall glass of mixed grapefruit and orange juices, the beverage she ordered regularly at this restaurant. Peter asked no questions. Instead, he politely removed the untouched alcoholic drink and replaced it with her usual one.

"Ladies, dinner will be ready soon," Peter informed the two women. They nodded to their waiter politely, not realizing that he had placed their dinner order for them that night.

"Sabera, this story has to be told from the beginning. Turquoise getting fired yesterday is not the end," Teal revealed as she sipped her cold mixed drink. "She almost got killed by a Mack truck the week before," sobbed Teal to her friend. Sabera looked at Teal's face to see tears mingling with her ice cubes.

"Oh, no — how?" Sabera said, in disbelief.

Teal daintily blew her nose.

Teal struggled to say, "Sh ... sh ... she was saved by a stranger who pulled her to safety." She reached into her purse to pull out a second tissue. Teal silently stared out into the empty space of the crowded restaurant.

The terrible tales about Turquoise were temporarily halted when the waiter walked by. Peter placed the piping-hot platters of salmon and steamed vegetables on the red cotton tablecloth. The distress of the moment dissipated.

Teal turned her head and looked directly into Sabera's encouraging eyes.

"What are you going to do to help your daughter?" beseeched Sabera.

Teal's faraway gaze now focused on the issue at hand and answered, "I think it's time for Turquoise to reconnect with our traditional ways of discipline and thinking," announced Teal. Adding a firm note, Teal confessed, "Roy and I have made a decision for Turquoise."

Teal moved closer to whisper the solution into Sabera's perfect-pitch musician's ear, "We are sending her to the Southwest. We sat down with Turquoise yesterday evening, and she agreed to decline her acceptance at PDQE College.

"I called Sierra Real University earlier today, and they have tentatively accepted her based on my telling the Registrar that Turquoise was the 2006 Valedictorian at Hawthorne Hills High School.

"Later, I called the High School to have Turquoise's transcript sent to the college via Express Mail.

"Frankly, Sabera, I was gratified at how well Turquoise took our 'recommendation' for her. She seemed almost relieved. We had essentially made the decision for her. She looked us both in the eyes and sighed, 'Thanks, Mom and Dad; I hope this change will be a new beginning for me. I can't go on like this; it's destroying my life.'"

Upon hearing Teal's response, Sabera signaled with agreement, "Y-e-a-h!!! I think this could be an invaluably wise decision for you and Roy and, of course, Turquoise."

26

Final Boarding Call

Just a little more than a month later, the final boarding calls were heard outside of the airline terminal. The Timerhorn family sprinted toward Gate 48 at Kennedy Airport. The sticky, humid August weather was left outside as they rushed into the air-conditioned boarding area.

Matthew Creek, Turquoise's fourteen-year-old brother, ran ahead and cried out to the flight attendant who was closing the Gate 48 door, "W-a-i-t, my sister has to get on board before you leave."

"Let's get a move on, young lady," ordered Roy Timerhorn to his middle child.

"Turquoise is not going away forever. She'll be back for Thanksgiving," Teal said as she patted Roy on his left shoulder.

Kissing and hugging her parents, she gave her sister Rita a peck on the left cheek. She saved her last hug for her former partner-in-crime, her younger brother, Matthew Creek, whom she adored.

Matthew Creek, a good listener, was the one who'd always helped Turquoise out of trouble. During the past year, he had set her alarm clock ahead an hour without her knowing it in an attempt to cure his sister's lateness habit. Now, he had prevented the jetway door to Gate 48 from closing. He would always be there for her.

Turquoise's last New York City sunset ended with tears falling across her cheeks like a gentle summer shower. She boarded the airplane without turning around for one last glance or waving good-bye. Unforeseen to Turquoise, this one-way airline ticket held her new destiny.

Rock Star of Lateness

Turquoise fastened her seat belt as the plane prepared to depart at 3:15 p.m. EDT. She took a pillow and nestled it behind her head. Then she settled in for her five-hour airplane ride to the Southwest. She dug into her pocketbook for a stick of sugarless gum and stumbled across an unopened letter addressed to her from Mrs. Windsong.

Turquoise pulled down the window shade to block out the intense summer sunrays. She began to read:

August 30th

My Dear Turquoise,

You are like the daughter I never had, but always wished I did. You are about to begin an important journey. Use every opportunity to grow and improve your life.

If you need help or advice, please call my cousin, Eva Knowing-Feather. Her number is 505-600-1444. She can help you on your quest. I've also taken the liberty of giving Eva your Aunt Sophie Mae's and Uncle Charlie's telephone number.

All my best,
Sabera Windsong

Returning the letter to its envelope, Turquoise slipped it back into her bag and smiled to herself. She thought, *"I'm going to call Ms. Knowing-Feather and make an appointment as soon as I get to my apartment. This high school graduate is determined to solve her punctuality dilemma. The riddle, once solved, can open many doors. In addition, it may be my entrance back into Edward's heart."*

The flight attendant came down the aisle to clear away the dinner trays. Some travelers were taking their shoes off, while others were preparing to view the in-flight movie. A businessman sitting across the aisle took out his company's survey report and began to read.

Turquoise blinked. She remembered painfully her recent exit and disgrace from Best Pharmaceutical Company. It had been just over a month since she was fired. Turquoise's wounds were still so raw that she found it difficult to focus on her future.

Turquoise's eyes welled up without warning. Tears streamed down her high cheekbones.

A young female passenger was sitting next to Turquoise. She gave Turquoise a tissue, not knowing or caring to know right then the reason for the tears, whether woeful or cheerful.

105

The traveler put her head on her personalized pillow. In the left-hand corner of the pillow were the traveler's initials monogrammed in golden threads. Her hair cascaded over the pillow to rival the brilliance of the silk monogram. With eyes shut a second later, she reclined into her aisle seat. Relaxation for the long ride was on everyone's mind, especially this traveler, a party-goer who had been up for almost twenty hours straight, but not so with Turquoise.

Laden with emotion, Turquoise turned to the unsuspecting sleeper on her left side. Flashing her alluring smile, she hoped to initiate a conversation with her seatmate.

"Excuse me, excuse me," Turquoise said to the exhausted passenger. From her window seat in row eighteen, Turquoise initiated a one-sided conversation. Turquoise hoped to release her emotional burden on a stranger. She continued her monologue. Unfortunately, the female passenger was ignoring Turquoise's words.

"Let me tell you what happened."

"Z-Z-Z-z-z. M-m-m-m—" groaned the unknown recipient of Turquoise's monologue. The groggy female traveler pretended not to hear Turquoise's persistent voice.

"Fired." said Turquoise. *"I can't believe I was fired!"* she blurted out in an agitated voice that had now taken hostage the ears of the stranger. The word "fired" seemed to arouse the curiosity of this slender youth. Her long eyelashes fluttered wide open. She blinked her lovely green eyes to adjust to the dimness of her surroundings.

With her interest now piqued, the airplane passenger inquired, "Why were you fired?" Fully awake now, the young lady interrogated Turquoise like a detective, hot on the trail for more clues.

"You see, about a month ago, I was still working at a New York pharmaceutical company. It was supposed to be my summer job. I was planning on finishing my job at the end of August and then going on to a college in New York."

Waving her hand up in the air, back and forth, the unidentified passenger now turned detective cried out, "Stop! Answer this simple question for me: Why did they fire you?"

"For lateness," Turquoise said as her head drooped and her chin touched her chest. Her usual sparkling eyes were dull.

"What did they say when you got fired?" inquired the stranger.

"My boss told me that I was a great worker. In fact, he praised my organizational skills. The Human Resource Director, Ms. London, told my er-er-er, let's say, 'my ex-boss,' how creative I was," mentioned Turquoise to her now eager listener.

Shaking her head in disbelief, Turquoise's listener turned her face away from the young lady who had poured her heart out to her. *Why is she telling me these things? 'Ms. London,' 'New York,' her tales of lateness*, the puzzled listener asked herself.

The young lady felt compelled to offer her advice. She turned her head back to her downcast seatmate, who now had a welcoming smile. The listener attempted to provide guidance.

"How many times were ...?" asked the girl, who was about the same age as Turquoise.

Being a good talker but not a great listener, Turquoise continued to extol her virtues. "All of my supervisors gave me top ratings."

As Turquoise paused a moment to catch her breath, the young lady took the opportunity to pursue her unanswered question. "How many times were you late to your job?" the traveler inquired again, impatiently.

Lowering her voice to a hum, "Out of five days," Turquoise confessed — she turned her gaze directly into the eyes of this person, searching for a sympathetic reaction — and admitted, "I usually went to work late four out of five days." Turquoise unloaded her emotions right into the unsuspecting ear of this listener.

"Are you kidding me? You were able to make it to work on time only once every five days?"

Turquoise nodded her head silently, confirming her seat-mate's accusation.

"Do you know who you are?" the stranger insisted.

"Yes. My name is Turquoise Nez Timerhorn."

"No, I don't mean your given first name and last name."

"Then, what name are you referring to?"

"I would call you 'The Rock Star of Lateness,'" the listener said to Turquoise with a concerned look on her face.

"Wow — no one has ever said that to me before."

Coming from a family with a strong work ethic and a focus on punctuality, the listener couldn't fully comprehend this reply. However, she pondered a moment to give credit to this person who had spoken openly about her pain and anguish at being fired due to her tardiness.

She deliberately softened her tone. "Hey, it's not the end of the world. Stay focused on what you are doing. Ignore the distractions, and do only one thing at a time," said this soon-to-be friend.

"Yeah, you're right. Sometimes, I do get carried away with my curiosity. I must pay attention to the time, especially if I have an appointment — and forget the interruptions," Turquoise summarized aloud what the listener had just said.

Drained from releasing her tidal wave of shame and guilt, Turquoise sat very still in her seat. Her long, raven hair was held in place by ribbons. She removed the ribbons, allowing her hair to fall loosely to one side of her shoulder. She felt free from pain for the first time in weeks.

Circumstances always prevailed that prevented me from arriving on time. I will never give up until I solve this punctuality puzzle. Now I realize how valuable the prize is, Turquoise thought to herself. She vowed silently, as she looked at the empathetic young woman beside her, not to lose another friendship because of lateness.

Without speaking further, she took a deep breath and slowly breathed out. On flight 826, Turquoise had gotten a chance to air out some of her disappointment.

In contrast, the listener with the long, blonde hair queried herself, *'Ms. London.' 'Ms. London.' That name rings a bell.*

The flight attendants were passing out beverages. The plane had just flown over St. Louis. It was around two-and-a-half hours from Albuquerque, New Mexico. Noticing the beauty and charm of these two young ladies, the lively flight attendant interrupted their conversation. "What would you like to drink?" she asked.

A second later the flight attendant set the two drinks down on the individual trays then moved aside to allow a striking young man to walk by.

"Hey, did you see that incredibly good-looking guy?" Turquoise's seatmate whispered in disbelief.

"You mean that one — the one with the shoulder-length ponytail?" Turquoise asked as she turned to the next page of her college catalogue. "I only saw his hair — not his face," Turquoise related to her new acquaintance, unimpressed.

After a midflight conversation of a few hours, the pair discovered that they were enrolled at the same college in New Mexico.

Turquoise was now focused on her new school, Sierra Real University. She had never had her own apartment before. Her late registration had necessitated her living off-campus. Her parents had arranged for her to stay at the Alta Mesa Apartment Complex in Albuquerque, New Mexico.

"You know something?" Turquoise blurted. "We've been busy talking this whole flight, and I've never asked your name."

Extending her hand to shake her seatmate's, the initiator of the conversation, said calmly again, "I'm Turquoise Nez Timerhorn. You can call me 'Turquoise.'"

"I'm Jane," said Turquoise's seatmate, pausing before adding, "Jane Best."

"Now, isn't that a coincidence. I was fired from the Best Pharmaceutical Company," Turquoise half-heartedly laughed. "There is a 'Mr. Best' who is the CEO at that firm."

Tapping with two fingers on the left side of her face, Turquoise asked the inevitable question, "Hey — he isn't any relation to you, Jane, is he?' Turquoise was feeling cautious as she shifted to turn and look directly at Jane.

Wasting no time, Jane delivered the missile-like answer on target, admitting, "Oh, he's just my dad," she casually stated.

With the landing gear engaged and the "Fasten Seat Belt " sign on, Turquoise noticed — a little bit too late — the inscription on Jane's burgundy-and-gold pen as she wrote down her name and address for Turquoise — "Best Pharmaceutical Company®"

Turquoise was chagrined beyond belief as she reflected upon this latest revelation. The disturbing news of Jane's identity left Turquoise dumbfounded. She evaded her present embarrassment as she mingled with the other passengers disembarking the plane.

The Road Ahead

The flight landed smoothly at the Albuquerque airport. It signaled multiple beginnings. The desert sun had already set. The Moon family impatiently awaited the arrival of their New York relative, Turquoise.

Teal Timerhorn's sister, Sophie Mae, welcomed Turquoise by throwing her arms around her. She released Turquoise in order to examine her niece from head to toe.

The next words out of Aunt Sophie Mae's mouth reminded Turquoise of her mission. "It's so good to see you, Turquoise. I'm so happy you will be attending college out here." With a worried glance, she turned to her husband thinking, *My little late bird*. Teal, her sister, had shared numerous long-distance conversations about the recent crises in Turquoise's life. Her disturbing accounts still resounded in her ears: nearly getting killed in New York City traffic and being fired from an excellent summer job.

"Yes, welcome, Turquoise," her uncle, Charlie Moon, added to lighten the awkwardness of the moment.

"It's wonderful to visit you guys here," said Turquoise, realizing she hadn't spoken to her cousin.

"Yeah — this time, you can stay in my room," Topaz declared. "When I come to New York to visit you, I share your room," she added.

The words "New York" reminded Turquoise about the letter that she had in her purse. Tired from being pulled out of bed earlier that day to catch her plane to New Mexico, Turquoise decided to put off making the phone call to Mrs. Windsong's cousin, Eva. Turquoise was exhausted.

The Moon family drove along the road. Peering out the car window, Turquoise felt calmed by her new surroundings. The road ahead told her that she was traveling away from the artificial lights of the airport. Turquoise leaned her head against the back seat of the car and glanced out at the bright night sky. *The stars are like permanent lamps that can show you the way home*, Turquoise thought to herself.

They finally arrived in front of the Moons' spacious home. Their neighborhood brushed the outskirts of the Albuquerque city limits by ten miles. Turquoise took in the fresh aroma of unpolluted air.

Maybe, it might not be so bad being here in New Mexico after all, even though I didn't have much of a choice, Turquoise silently rationalized to herself.

She knew good and well that she was being put through a "rite of passage" by her parents. Turquoise could no longer be treated like a child. She had to learn how to be an adult, with all of the responsibilities and privileges. Turquoise's aunt and uncle would be her mentors.

29

Hours of Your Time

During the next week, Turquoise shopped for items for her first apartment away from home. Turquoise wandered around Albuquerque, feeling the desert sun on her back and arms. The thermometer swelled to more than ninety-six degrees as she tried to become accustomed to the heat.

"The sunsets are more spectacular here than in New York," Turquoise exclaimed as she sat nightly on her uncle-and-aunt's front porch. She watched the red fireball drop down in the sky to create a blazing crimson horizon.

On the next morning, September 1st, she meandered down the sun-drenched Southwestern street. *Bong! Bong! Bong!* Turquoise heard the church bells strike eleven o'clock. Intrigued by the variety of stores, she stumbled upon one with the name "An Hour of Your Time." Swinging the heavy wooden door open, she ventured into a curiosity shop full of timekeeping pieces from different eras.

"Howdy," welcomed Octavia Crawford, owner of the clock store, which was located on Frontier Street and One Minute Boulevard.

"Hi. I'm just looking around," Turquoise stated in her smooth New York accent.

"Fine with me," encouraged Octavia in a Western twang. Octavia was a stocky woman with thick, wavy, silver hair. Octavia circulated throughout the store, helping several other customers make their timepiece selections. Glancing down at the silver-and-turquoise watch on her left wrist, she noted the time. It was 11:14 a.m.

Two men entered the store. They inquired about shipping three clocks to Florida and two to England. Octavia took out the packing boxes, preparing the purchases for domestic and international shipping.

Octavia Crawford paused to catch her breath from the whirlwind shopping spree of the stream of customers purchasing the fine clocks in her store. Octavia, an active person, was a native of seventy-two years to the rich red clay soil of New Mexico.

She sat effortlessly into the store's rocking chair. As she glanced up over the rim of her frameless glasses, she noticed that the young lady who had entered at 11:14 a.m. was still there at 12:04 p.m. This young lady obviously loved to browse.

"What can I help you with today?" this woman with broad shoulders and a pleasant twang to her voice asked her potential customer as she rose from the rocking chair.

"You really have a 'mean' collection of watches and clocks," complimented Turquoise.

"'Mean'?" asked Octavia as she moved to stand in front of the stranger. "Oh — do you want to say, perhaps, that you like my clock store?" Octavia suddenly realized the double meaning and laughed heartily. Her body shook like warm pudding on her 170-pound, 5' 4" frame.

"I'm a little scared of starting college here in September," Turquoise confessed.

"I need a very loud alarm clock," Turquoise admitted as she looked intently into Octavia's dark brown eyes. "I have trouble ... um-umm ...," Turquoise hesitated to finish her sentence.

"Waking up in the morning?" Octavia Crawford completed the sentence for the young lady, who was clearly no longer a baby.

"How did you know?" queried Turquoise.

"I wouldn't be in this business if I couldn't help people," chuckled the older woman, who felt like she had heard it all at her age.

"Well, maybe you can help me. I'm getting my own apartment next week, and I need an alarm clock that can ..." Turquoise thought for a moment before going on, "... can literally throw me out of the bed."

"What do you mean, dear, 'Throw you out of the bed'?" Octavia asked. Wrinkles creased her forehead while she folded her arms across her chest and tilted her head in puzzlement.

"I'm afraid I might be late when I start college. I begin classes at Sierra Real University on September 12th. I'm not at my best in the morning when I hear the alarm clock," Turquoise revealed as she drew the storeowner deeper into her world.

"That's easy — just buy yourself a good alarm clock," stated Octavia, frivolously as she walked behind the glass counter. Knowing a story was about to follow, she adjusted her right hearing aid to tune into the tale from this trim youth.

"I already have *five* alarm clocks!" Turquoise blurted out, losing her patience for a second, "… and none of them throws me out of bed."

"Just hold on there, *sugar* — no need to fret," Octavia said in a motherly, almost doctor-like tone to soothe this distressed soul. Meanwhile, Octavia didn't want this difficult shopper to frighten away other customers who were in the store.

Octavia glided out from behind the counter. She approached the upset beauty. Octavia Crawford moved slowly but with a definite purpose in mind. She gingerly touched Turquoise's elbow and guided her toward the center counter in the store. Once there, Octavia pointed out a clock with a large halogen bulb.

"No, not that," rejected Turquoise, insistently.

"Well, how about that clock over there, then?" continued Octavia, a bit irritated after glancing at her watch. It was now 2:24 p.m.

"That looks good. I see that the clock is in the shape of a little schoolhouse," Turquoise declared in a calmer voice than before. She examined the top and bottom of the clock. Next she tried the alarm. However, lost in her own thoughts, Turquoise stopped in the middle of the floor. She stood still and touched her ears, as if she were waiting to hear an answer to her punctuality dilemma.

"Did that ring loud enough for you, dear?" Octavia inquired.

A half an hour later, the determined Turquoise was still searching around in the store for the perfect alarm clock — the one that would force her to be on time.

Octavia thought over the conversation she had just had with this freshman college student. Octavia followed her around the store and saw that perspiration droplets were forming on her nose.

She wants a clock that can 'throw her out of bed', Octavia challenged her mature mind. *She rejected my first, very good suggestion. Can I solve this customer's predicament?*

Then, Octavia had a moment in which she felt that an apple had suddenly fallen out of a tree and hit her on the head. An idea had inspired her.

Octavia, grateful for her breakthrough, spoke up and pierced the awkward silence.

"Put the alarm clock far away from where you are sleeping. In fact, put the alarm clock on the opposite side of your bed. In this way, you will be forced to get out of your bed to shut off the alarm," Octavia thoughtfully suggested.

"O-o-oh, thanks for that idea," squeaked Turquoise to Octavia. Octavia inhaled and exhaled an air of satisfaction. She swelled with the pride of a sphinx that had just solved the punctuality riddle of a desperate young lady hoping to cure her lateness.

Turquoise purchased the fifty-dollar schoolhouse clock. She cradled her new acquisition in her arms and strolled confidently out of the "An Hour of Your Time" store at 3:45 p.m. She presumed that she had discovered a solution to her tardiness problem.

Octavia waved good-bye to a stranger who had become like a friend. Ten minutes later, four new customers entered the store. Octavia contemplated, *Maybe I should change the name of my store from "An Hour of Your Time" to just plain "Hours."*

Turquoise was the kind of person who left a lasting impression on people she met. The clock-store owner realized she had never learned the young woman's name.

Survival Skill

Back home at her off-campus accommodations, Turquoise surveyed her bedroom to determine just where to place her new clock as far away from her bed as possible. Instantly, her thoughts drifted back to a memorable conversation she had had with her father several years ago which she had never forgotten.

"Daddy — how do you know when it is time to wake up in the morning? How do you arrive home at six o'clock every evening? How does Mommy know it is six o'clock even when she is not looking at a clock?" asked Turquoise, without pausing for a breath, as she badgered her father for answers. Turquoise knew that her father never wore a watch, yet he came home around 6:00 p.m. daily.

"Hold on, baby girl. You know, you are just eight years old, and you are drilling me for answers like you were an investigator. Trust me — I just know," said Roy. "I remember being told this by your grandmother Sarah Timerhorn, when I was a young child like you," spoke the father to his second-born child. He answered all of her questions with the patience of a parent guiding his child to an understanding of how things work in society.

Later on during the discussion, Turquoise's father retold the proud legacy of his parents, Sarah and Robert Timerhorn. It was an oral history that was once told to him by his parents. Now, the other two children, Rita and Matthew Creek, joined Turquoise on the sofa in the living room. They also wanted to listen and to learn from their father; a man who spoke with wisdom and a proud heritage that honored the natural environment and much more.

Looking at his three children, Roy spoke in a way that made them want to hear more. Roy's heart swelled with pride for his family. He was a great storyteller. Roy had learned this skill from his father. The older men kept the traditions alive by retelling their history as far back as they could remember.

Roy Timerhorn, a tall man with big shoulders, could pick up his three young children in his arms. He stood 6' 2" in his bare feet. He had a premature, frosted-silver patch of hair right in the front of his head. His appearance made him an unforgettable man, and his storytelling was legendary.

Roy was a warrior for promptness. His habit of punctual arrival, in spite of crowds, tornados, hurricanes, and unforeseen delays made him a more-than-remarkable person.

After dinner that night, he related a tale passed down in his family from one generation to the next. Roy's eyes moved slowly toward his left. Then they darted quickly in the opposite direction.

"This is what my elders told me when I was a boy — a story about the eternal odyssey of the sun crossing the sky every day," Roy began. Using his right hand and arm to signal the movement, Roy continued, "We now know the earth makes its orbit around the sun. Nevertheless, this same phenomenon was observed by The First People, long before Christopher Columbus arrived on the shores of our lands ...."

Remembering his own childhood, Roy remained silent for a moment, giving honor to past generations who fought to be free on their own land and knowing that the real struggle continued even today. Roy wanted to pass on knowledge and the truth that was not yet written in the standard history books.

The three spellbound children sat motionless on the comfortable sofa.

"The joy of the sunrise delights me," whispered Roy to the next generation of Timerhorns. "I've never used a clock or a watch to wake me up. My 'biological clock,' as they call it now, works very well for me. Modern instruments such as watches were not necessary for ancient folks."

A tiny Turquoise voice asked, "Why, Daddy?"

The storyteller continued, "The Creator has given us a special gift. It is also called 'circadian rhythm.' It is the natural body clock that helps us all to determine time. For example, some people are active in the morning, or they have great energy during the afternoon. Other people have great strength and creative thinking power during the evening," explained Roy to his children, who were in awe as he spoke.

He added, "We are social beings, as well, and our individual time rhythms must essentially agree with and respect the time patterns of those among whom we share this earth, sky and sun."

Teal entered the living room and stood behind the sofa. She never interrupted her husband during moments like this. The purple-and-golden horizon told Teal that the children's bedtime was near.

Roy automatically understood her signal. He quickly glanced out the window and saw the sun completing its path. The fiery orange ball was barely visible, sinking below the summer horizon. The Timerhorn family enjoyed the sunset together every evening. It was their cherished family time together.

Gazing out of the other window in the living room, Roy pointed with his left hand. "The time markers at night are the moon and the stars. Time is a precious gift. Look deep inside yourselves, my children."

Then, adding a private thought of encouragement to Turquoise, he said, "You are a champion, soaring like an eagle with the strength, courage, and power to arrive early on whichever path you travel."

Finally, Roy targeted a question particularly to his second daughter. "Have I answered your question?" asked this patient father. He knew that his daughter Turquoise would experience pain unless she learned this crucial survival skill.

31

Where Should I Put This Clock?

Turquoise's reminiscence shifted to her mother. Roy's wife, Teal, had been a loving and devoted parent. She was also punctual for all of her appointments. When the children were young, Teal always took them to and from school. The school staff never had to wait for her to pick them up. Teal was always there on time.

Teal had the habit of wearing a different watch each day. She liked to match the color of the watch to the clothing she was wearing.

"Please, run to my jewelry box and bring me my watch, Turquoise," instructed Teal to her daughter one day.

It had been a year since Turquoise's father told her why he didn't use a watch. Teal enjoyed wearing watches as jewelry. She had more than a dozen watches in her timepiece collection.

Turquoise, then at age nine, still remembered the night that her father, the storyteller, had told her about time. She carefully picked up a watch. It had a lemon-colored elastic wristband with Roman numerals on the face. She gave it to her mother to wear.

"No, not that one, sweetheart," Turquoise's mother gently chided her daughter. "I am wearing a red suit," Teal told her daughter, who didn't know how to coordinate colors yet.

Turquoise had been standing in her parents' bedroom. She reached again into her mother's jewelry box. This time, she took out a watch that had the numbers twelve, three, six, and nine on the face along with a red leather wristband. Her mother tried this second watch on and smiled.

As a youngster of nine years, Turquoise had come to a naive conclusion after a minute. She thought to herself, *Maybe you can be on time if you buy a watch to match the color of your outfit.* Next, Turquoise asked, "Mommy, can you and Daddy buy me a watch?"

"Is that what you want for your next birthday?" Teal searched Turquoise's face for clues.

"Yes. My birthday is coming soon. I want to start a collection like yours, Mommy," Turquoise said, happily.

Teal Timerhorn nodded with a smile. It was a small request. "Hmm," Teal smiled to herself silently. *Perhaps a watch would help Turquoise learn to become aware of time for herself.*

Much had changed in the fifteen years that Teal had been married to Roy Timerhorn. Teal had always wanted to finish her master's degree in business administration. Having three small children prevented her, temporarily, from going back to school.

She made a telephone call to a local college. While she was waiting for someone to answer, she did some mathematical calculations for herself.

Now, Rita is eleven. Turquoise will be ten, and Matthew Creek is no longer the baby boy in diapers. He's seven years old ...

Clearing her throat to speak firmly into the telephone, Teal, for the first time, saw a way to work outside of the home. "Would you please send me your Graduate School catalog at ..."

Five years after that college catalog arrived, Teal Timerhorn achieved her goal. Four-and-a-half satisfying, yet demanding, years of being a wife, a mother, and a part-time student at college had paid off.

Recently Roy had declared affectionately to his wife, "At last, I have you to myself — my sweet MBA graduate."

"My tender sparrow, I don't want to alarm you, but ... I am concerned about ..." Roy commented to his wife.

Teal completed her husband's sentence with one word: "Turquoise?" as she touched her favorite turquoise choker, which she always wore.

"The reason I'm bringing up the subject is that I overheard our children talking," related Roy.

Teal responded, "They don't talk, Roy, they usually argue with each other. Tsk-tsk. Children will be children," Teal commented as she dismissed Roy's concerns.

"No, no, listen to me," Roy urged Teal. "Our son, Matthew Creek, told his sister Rita about an incident he had with his friend who saw Turquoise last Monday."

Teal yawned nonchalantly and questioned, "Well, what happened to her?"

Roy positioned his arms like a bird in flight. Then he repeated exactly what Matthew Creek, their twelve-year-old son, had told Rita: "Hey Matt — who is that flying down the street to catch the bus?" said Matthew Creek's friend while he was standing at the bus stop.

In storytelling fashion, Roy's voice rose higher to reflect the climax of the tale. "Our son replied to his friend, 'Unfortunately, that's my ... sister ... RUNNING LATE for the bus, again.'"

Continuing, Roy tried to hide his consternation. "Our son later told me that his classmates teased him about Turquoise galloping down the street. That's no way for a young lady to behave," Roy sermonized to Teal.

Turquoise painfully recalled overhearing her parents' conversation that day. The juxtaposition of the memory of those past incidents with her all too recent fiascos was temporarily halted by a flashing light that returned her to present reality. The battery was charged. "Where should I put this clock?"

32

Off on the Wrong Foot

No one could have expected how "coincidence and punctuality" would play a part in bringing about an unlikely alliance.

Settled in her dorm, Jane Best went to visit Turquoise's spacious, two-bedroom, off-campus apartment on September 5th. Turquoise's parents had reserved this convenient furnished apartment near the campus. It was three blocks from Sierra Real University.

Both girls arrived on time for registration. Turquoise noticed the similarities between Jane and "her Edward." Turquoise thought to herself while she waited on line to pay for her classes. *Huh — Jane really knows how to get around. She's her father's daughter. That was an important tip she gave me back on the plane: "Stay focused."*

Remembering to restrain her curiosity, which often caused her to go off the path for an adventure, Turquoise managed to keep up with her new college friend, Jane Best, heiress to a multibillion dollar pharmaceutical company.

Later that afternoon at the Alta Mesa Apartment Complex, the two coeds got a chance to share their programs.

"What time is your first class on September 12th?" Jane asked Turquoise as Turquoise put her favorite books on the bookshelves in her bedroom.

From her bedroom, Turquoise retorted, "8:00 a.m. And yours?" Turquoise put away her three new Sierra Real University t-shirts in her dresser drawer while waiting for Jane's response.

"Seven o'clock — rise and shine," responded Jane, trained by her father to be an early riser.

Turquoise whispered to herself, "Whew. Aren't you the early bird!"

During those last few days of summer freedom, Jane flew back to New York the weekend before classes began to be with her father. Turquoise, however, visited her Uncle Charlie and Aunt Sophie Mae.

Topaz Moon, Turquoise's seventeen-year-old cousin, asked her streetwise New York relative if she wanted to go shopping with her. Unable to resist, Turquoise's voice vibrated a monosyllable word, "Yes!"

"Which store should we start with?" asked Topaz as she pulled out her list of seven items that she wanted to buy from Teen-Tops Clothes Emporium.

"'An Hour of Your Time' must be our first stop," Turquoise insisted while she brushed her hair into place.

"I'm looking forward to the privileges of being a senior this year," said Topaz Moon, excitedly, to her cousin who had just graduated from high school.

"But being a college freshman is better," bragged Turquoise.

"Hey, cousin, I forgot to tell you that somebody named 'Eva' called here the other night looking for you," Topaz snapped back.

"Oh, no! I missed my appointment with Mrs. Windsong's cousin," said Turquoise, regretfully, as she slapped her forehead. "I must have stayed too long in that clock store last week."

Topaz sharpened her high school senior killer-instinct in a battle of wits against a college freshman. She reprimanded her older cousin by saying, "Obviously, you didn't get the right clock if you missed your appointment."

"Don't play with me," Turquoise retorted in a menacing tone to her cousin Topaz. "Your mother has trusted me with a substantial amount of money to use for *our* purchases today," Turquoise, the cutthroat spender, shot back in retaliation to Topaz's comment.

Topaz Moon, who was two inches shorter than her 5' 7" New York cousin, just glared at Turquoise. Topaz then mustered up the one word that would break the growing tension. She mumbled softly, "Sorry."

"That's alright, Topaz," Turquoise quickly answered. A moment of silence gave Turquoise a chance to sort out what had just transpired between the two cousins.

The final verdict in Turquoise's head was *she's tough, but fair.* Turquoise realized that her cousin's comment did have an important element of truth in it: Turquoise *had* missed her appointment with Eva.

To camouflage the uncomfortable balance of power, Turquoise proclaimed, "Before we go shopping today, please give me a minute right now to call Eva and apologize," Turquoise stated in a bashful voice.

As she moved toward the telephone, Turquoise said over her shoulder, "I love you, Topaz, even if you are a pain in the neck." Then she turned around and smiled congenially.

Don't kill the messenger because of the message, Topaz thought to herself. She listened as her cousin Turquoise employed wild excuses and half-truths to explain to Ms. Knowing-Feather, over the telephone, why she had missed her 2:00 p.m. appointment last week. Turquoise carefully avoided telling Ms. Knowing-Feather the truth — that she had been in a clock store for more than four hours.

33

Wait Until Next Month

Octavia Crawford immediately recognized the smile, the pretty face, and the long, glistening hair of the loquacious customer, still a nameless client. She had just rolled into the 'An Hour of Your Time' store again, this time, with a sidekick. An irksome voice drifted into Octavia's ears.

"Hi, there — I'm b-a-c-k."

"Yes, you sure are," said Octavia while she muttered under her breath, "Is it a blue moon?" She didn't realize that she had spoken her thoughts a little too loud.

Topaz asked the storeowner, "How did you know my last name is Moon?"

"Huh? 'Moon'? Well, er, well, er ...." Then, remembering how the young college student had captivated her the first time they'd met, Octavia imitated Turquoise's style. "Well, let me introduce myself — I'm Octavia Crawford, owner of this unique clock store. We mail clocks and treasured timepieces all over the world," said Octavia, trying to cover her tracks.

"I'm Topaz Moon, and this is my cousin from New York, Turquoise Nez Timerhorn."

"Howdy — what can I do for you two today before I close for my lunch break?" Octavia inquired as she checked her watch. It was nearly twelve o'clock. Octavia Crawford, successful storeowner, scratched her wavy silver hair. She wondered to herself, *How long will it take her today to buy a clock? With my luck, we'll both be here 'til midnight.* Octavia, whose joy in life was running the store, laughed inwardly at her predicament.

Octavia's late husband, Ezekiel Crawford, had picked out the name for the store. They had joyously shared more than thirty years of owning it together. Now it had been two years since he'd left her embrace — not for another woman but to meet his Maker.

Octavia and "Zeke," a name Octavia used affectionately when addressing her husband, had never had any children. Zeke would tell Octavia that his love for her was wider than the Rocky Mountains. They could fill their store with love, welcoming every person who entered it.

In effect, the store had become the child Octavia and Zeke never had. Octavia spent hard-working hours to make the store special. The perpetual ticking of the clocks reminded her of Zeke's heart when she would lay her head across his chest. Octavia carried on her late husband's legacy of helping customers find exactly what they wanted. Zeke used to tell Octavia every night, "Time is a treasure, if it is used wisely." Octavia recalled those precious evenings when the sky began to darken into swirls of cinnamon, azure blue, and lavender on the horizon.

Now Octavia attended the two shoppers as they leisurely walked around the clock store. Once again, Octavia was drawn into the conversation.

"I would like to buy that clock with the halogen bulb you showed me before. That advice you gave me the last time, Ms. Crawford, really paid off big time," exclaimed Turquoise, smiling.

"Fine — I'll wrap it up securely!" Octavia said delightedly.

"Please explain again how it works exactly," Turquoise asked before Octavia closed the box.

Octavia began to demonstrate how the clock was designed to awaken the reluctant riser. "It has no snooze button," she stated. "It awakens you by light. It takes about a half an hour to wake you gently by growing brighter and brighter every five minutes," instructed Octavia as she gently moved the hands on the clock. "Plus, it has a nurturing ring to help wake you up," Octavia pointed out, hoping to clinch the sale. "The alarm rings after the halogen bulb completes its cycle."

"I'll take it. I'll take it," Turquoise blurted out as she bounced up and down with glee. This latest purchase would become the pinnacle of her growing alarm-clock collection.

Topaz continued to explore the store while Ms. Crawford wrapped up the clock for her customer, whose name she now knew — and, by accident, the unusual last name of her relative.

Turquoise thought to herself, *I know I can do it now. I can be on time. School starts on the twelfth, and I'll be ready.*

And she was.

The very next week, Turquoise arrived at college at 7:45 a.m. each morning for her 8:00 a.m. class in business practices. Sophie Mae Moon called her sister to report the good news.

"My husband and I check in on her every other day," beamed Sophie Mae, the monitor, reporting to her skeptical sister, Teal.

"Yeah, yeah, yeah, sister dear — it's only been three weeks," warned Teal.

"Well, I'm optimistic. Turquoise has a persevering streak that will serve her well. She's determined to overcome what she is now calling 'My Punctuality Dilemma,'" Sophie Mae informed her sister.

There was an awkward silence between the (505) and (718) area codes on the telephone connection.

Teal hung up the telephone by saying, "The final report is not in. Let's see what will happen next month, in October. It's still only the beginning of the semester now. Bye, Sophie Mae."

34

I'll Bounce Back

On an early October morning, Turquoise returned to her apartment after spending the night out at her cousin Topaz's house. She took the mail out of the mailbox in the lobby. She noticed that the return address on the envelope was from New York City. Turquoise didn't take the elevator to reach her second-floor apartment, 2A.

Instead, Turquoise walked up the one flight of stairs. Holding onto the railing as she maneuvered her way one step at a time, Turquoise anxiously ripped the envelope open and read the letter.

October 2nd,

Hi Turquoise,
*   How are you doing in school? I miss you. So does*
the whole crew. Valerie is taking a psychology class at the
College of Human Studies. She is driving all of us nuts
trying to analyze our personalities.
*   Griffin is a big basketball star at Staten Island*
University. His picture recently appeared in the local
newspapers. Valerie was so proud of her honey that she
bought out the whole newsstand. Now, who do you think
needs an analyst, her or Griffin? (LOL).
*   Colón finally decided on the Air Force in order to*
pursue a career in aviation. He hopes to see the world. I
haven't heard from him since last week, but maybe he will
call me soon. I guess they're keeping him busy in training.
*   I ran into Jonathan Quincy and Natasha Orlov at*
the mall. They were shopping for matching winter jackets.
Did you know that they are both going for premed? Boy,
who would have thought sitting next to them in biology
would turn into a love affair of the liver, pancreas, and
lungs? Yuck!
*   I've written enough. I will bring you up to speed*
when I write to you again. Gotta go! The phone is ring-
ing, and it could be my man in uniform.

BFF,
Becky

Turquoise finally reached apartment 2A. She inserted the key and unlocked the door. There was still a P.S. closing note to Becky Córpuz's letter.

Checking her watch to see if she had time to finish reading the unexpected letter from her best friend, Turquoise entered her bedroom. She tilted the venetian blinds, allowing the warm New Mexican morning rays to flood her bedroom.

She gently fingered the silver-and-turquoise necklace she still wore in remembrance of her Edward.

Turquoise reclined on top of her Southwestern-patterned comforter. She held the letter close to her eyes as if to squeeze more information out of it.

She began to read Becky's postscript.

P.S. I know you want an update on Ed. Well, that new girlfriend, Stephanie Strong, who we all thought was definitely wrong for Ed, actually made our July party at the beach enjoyable. On Labor Day, she and Ed hung out with us at the South Street Seaport. Plus, I am sending you an e-mail that has Ed and Stephanie's picture from our graduation. She uploaded it online with an update to her status — "In a Relationship."

P.P.S. I'll keep in touch. It's Colón, on the phone. See ya'.

Restraining her tears, Turquoise did the next best thing. She rose from the bed and walked over to a chair. Then she plopped down for what seemed like an eternity. Peering up at the wooden clock over her bed, Turquoise consciously decided to skip college that day.

Sitting motionless in her chair for what seemed like hours, she gently opened the catch on the silver-and-turquoise necklace she was wearing. It held so many memories of Edward. Turquoise stood up and walked slowly over to the window. Next, she intentionally dropped the necklace on the windowsill behind the venetian blinds. After seeing Ed and Stephanie's graduation picture, she had lost all hope of being in Ed's life again.

She thought to herself, *I will leave it here. The next time I touch it, I will push it out the window. That way, I can forget Edward Windsong, who dumped me because, I …*

Suddenly, the phone rang and jolted Turquoise out of her painful reminiscence. She blinked and said to herself, "Who can that be?"

"Hello, Turquoise?" said an oversweet, male voice on the other end of the telephone.

"Oh, hi, Tyler," Turquoise muttered nonchalantly into the receiver.

"I'm just checking on you. I missed you. I gave my presentation in Professor Ackerman's business class today."

Tyler O'Boerum, a young man with wavy red hair and dark freckles on his face, was intrigued by his classmate's distinctive smile. He paused a second before asking meekly, "Why were you absent from school today, Turquoise?" Tyler had taken it upon himself to look out for a fellow scholar he was smitten by.

Avoiding a direct answer, Turquoise responded with a slight irritation in her voice. "I'll see you tomorrow, Tyler, at 8:00 a.m. when I'll make my presentation in Professor Ackerman's class. Thanks for calling. See ya!" Turquoise expressed her annoyance by hanging up the telephone abruptly without hearing Tyler's words of good-bye.

Turning on her late-model computer, Turquoise began to assemble her business masterpiece. She typed nonstop for an hour before resting.

Turquoise returned to her computer at 7:00 p.m. She mapped out her introduction, her plan of action, and her conclusion for the project that was due at 8:00 a.m. on the following day.

At 10:27 p.m., Turquoise decided that she would print out her paper in the morning. She wandered into the living room to watch the ten o'clock news, which was already on. Feeling a little drained from the emotional roller coaster of Becky's letter and e-mail, Turquoise decided to go to bed early.

She had been forced to confront her own feelings that she had buried when she left New York. Turquoise couldn't hold back any longer the crystal tears streaming down on her cheeks.

Then, Turquoise stepped silently out of the living room toward her bedroom, muttering aloud, "No more excuses. All I need is a good night's sleep. I will bounce back."

35

Good Luck, Gorgeous

The following morning, Turquoise paced back and forth in her bedroom. She could not make that printer go any faster. She thought that the thirty-page report would take but a few minutes to print. Nevertheless, she had to wait more than twenty minutes. In the middle of printing, she had to replace the ink cartridge, very grateful that she had one. However, Turquoise had to search for more paper. Discovering that she had none, she went to borrow some from a student who lived next door. Turquoise glanced at her watch and realized that it was almost 8:07 a.m.

Turquoise's mind didn't have to race to do the mathematical calculations. "I am now good and late!"

With an all-too-familiar dash, Turquoise rushed from her apartment to run to school.

With a kick and a bang, the door to Professor Ackerman's class swung open. It was 8:31 a.m. on October 8th. All of her classmates were startled by the sudden disturbance Turquoise had created.

Springing into the room, the excuse-laden Turquoise began to babble excitedly.

"Professor Ackerman, I'm sorry. I'm a little late. I didn't realize that printing thirty pages would take s-o-o-o long," she confessed as she handed her professor a copy of the presentation.

"Just start your presentation, *Ms. Timerhorn*." Professor Ackerman snapped curtly. "We are *all* waiting for you to begin."

Hurriedly smoothing down her business suit, Turquoise took a deep breath and started. She scanned the audience for friendly faces. Her eyes fell upon an arresting male.

His rugged profile and sunbathed skin heightened his aristocratic aura as his eyes shined like two black pearls.

His smile was a reaction to the attractive but harried latecomer. It highlighted his full, firm lips neatly tucked under a trim mustache. He was seated in the front row of the one-hundred-seat lecture hall. His friendly face seemed to silently project, "Good luck, gorgeous!"

Determined to give an outstanding presentation, Turquoise forged ahead, presuming that her tardiness had been overlooked.

"Good morning," Turquoise cheerfully launched her presentation.

Meanwhile, at the back of the auditorium, a student murmured, "You mean, 'Good afternoon.'"

Several students thought to themselves, *Good night!*

"My presentation is on 'Time Management,'" Turquoise declared boldly.

Professor Ackerman, chairperson of the Business Department, shook her head in disbelief.

Turquoise introduced her subject by stating, "We have probably all had the embarrassing experience of being late for an important appointment or meeting."

A student in the third row thought to himself, *Perhaps, but you were the only one late this morning for a presentation!*

Turquoise continued with her limited knowledge of this subject. "Do you find yourself making excuses for your lateness?"

Another classmate in the twelfth row on the left side of the lecture hall cringed and thought to herself, *What's your excuse today, you pretty little hypocrite?*

A male student took her last statement to heart and pondered, *I would never accept habitual lateness from my girlfriend. It is one thing to be late in a social setting — no more than five minutes. However, to roll in late on the day of your own presentation is unforgivable.*

I never had this issue in the way you've got it, foxy sister, thought another male student simultaneously.

Turquoise asserted, "I'm sure that we all will agree that a habitual lack of punctuality is disrespectful unless it is due to circumstances beyond your control."

How could any one person have so many situations beyond their control that would justify habitual lateness? This student is downright illogical, a philosophy major rationalized to herself. *I've got to make it a point to speak to her after class.*

Also perceiving the ironic ineptitude of Ms. Timerhorn's reasoning, Professor Ackerman began to assess the overall quality of this student's presentation. *This young lady will need some serious remediation in good business practices. Unfortunately, her charming manner won't matter in the world of high finance and business.*

As Turquoise was approaching the conclusion of her time-management presentation, she segued by saying, "I will now give you an overview of several solutions that are popular in self-help books on this subject."

Completely unaware of their inner thoughts, Turquoise employed her well-known smile to execute what she considered to be a polished ending, not realizing she had alienated much of her audience.

Tyler raced to Turquoise after class. He boldly flung his comments at her — "You did a good job!"

Turning around to read the faces of the other departing classmates, Turquoise locked eyes again with the mysterious, good-looking male classmate.

He slowly got up. Winking his right eye, he flashed a brilliant smile. Believing that this tall figure was flirting with her, Turquoise quickly turned away, bashfully, toward Tyler.

"How soon do you think that Professor Ackerman will give me my grade?" Turquoise questioned Tyler. "I know I was late getting to class, but my presentation was superior," she added.

Tyler O'Boerum didn't get the chance to answer Turquoise.

Professor Ackerman approached Turquoise from behind and addressed her query bluntly. "Here, Ms. Timerhorn!" and returned Turquoise's graded report immediately.

Professor Ackerman walked away from the scene of the disaster. Turquoise opened her report quickly. She searched each page for the grade. Seconds later, the remaining students in the room heard an outburst.

"What do you mean — 55?" Turquoise screeched over the professor's shoulder as Professor Ackerman walked toward the exit of the lecture hall.

Displaying a disconcerted frown, Turquoise blurted out audaciously, "Professor, my work was completed, my presentation was thorough, although I … was … a little late," justified Turquoise. Regaining her composure, Turquoise explained in a negotiating manner, "I believe I told you that my printer took longer than I expected."

"Unfortunately, Ms. Timerhorn, this is not open for discussion. But, I will tell you this: In business, you must factor in extra time when you are working on a project," advised Professor Ackerman. She added a final stinging comment to Turquoise: "Always be prepared — especially for the unexpected."

36

Devastated and Desolate

Standing in the doorway of reality, Turquoise, the academic whiz kid with a 98.9 percent high school average, tried to reconcile herself to the reasons for her failure. The professor swiftly exited the lecture hall, leaving one casualty behind.

Landing on the rough road of rock bottom, Turquoise turned back into the lecture hall to collect her belongings. Two female classmates approached Turquoise as she bent over to put her charts and handouts into her briefcase.

"Your information wasn't entirely pertinent and coherent," one student began.

"And, your late arrival totally compromised your integrity and credibility on the subject," interjected the other classmate. As they left, one of them remarked, "We hope you take this as friendly criticism. You have a very engaging manner."

Although her eyes were tearless, her heart was devastated and desolate. The criticism evoked a painful flashback in Turquoise's mind. *What's going on with me? I constantly compromise my reputation:*

* ❄ late for the prom
* ❄ lost the crown
* ❄ Edward left me
* ❄ late to work virtually every day
* ❄ almost killed rushing back to work after lunch
* ❄ fired by Mr. Best
* ❄ run out of town by my own parents
* ❄ and finally a 55 for my presentation on time management today

Sinking into a front-row seat in the lecture hall, Turquoise lowered her head into her hands. She murmured, "What will become of me? I have got to find an answer for my dilemma, and I don't know where to turn."

The hall was now deserted, but Turquoise sensed the presence of someone near her. Suddenly rising, she whirled around to stare directly at the 5' 11" broad-shouldered frame of a young man.

"You're still an A+ in my book!" he stated smoothly, in his deep voice.

"Thanks for the flattery, but I'm still an 'F' in the teacher's book," the coed sadly replied as her fetchingly wild curls bounced and flowed untamed down her back.

"May I cheer you up a little? Maybe we can plan some strategies over a cup of coffee?" articulated the dark-haired stranger with shoulder-length hair pulled back into a ponytail.

"Allow me to formally introduce myself: I am Dakota Blackfoot," declared the stranger in a majestic voice to the speechless Turquoise. His charm, along with his rugged good looks, distracted Turquoise from her anguish.

Nine minutes later, the two classmates arrived at a campus coffee house called "The Hot One." They were sitting directly opposite each other as if in a debate. Forty-five minutes into the conversation, the young man began sipping hazelnut coffee with Turquoise. No longer "the stranger" from her class, he began to unfold his story about his wink.

"So, Mr. Dakota Blackfoot," said Turquoise. "Do you flirt with every woman you meet with a wink?"

Smiling, he answered, "Unfortunately, a lot of people mistake my wink for flirting. But actually, I am not flirting," defended the twenty-five-year-old Dakota.

Smelling the natural musk cologne "Freedom" on this outdoorsy guy, Turquoise completely forgot her grade of 55 from the morning. She leaned over the hot brew resting on the small, round coffee table. She flashed her 100-watt smile at the handsome guy, who had a slight scar over his left eyebrow.

Nothing could detract from Dakota's good looks. A thin silver clasp on the lanyard tie around his collar highlighted a distinguished, debonair flair when he grinned. He oozed masculinity with his body language. His smile complemented Turquoise's.

Dakota leaned forward to push back Turquoise's wind-tossed hair. Now, he could admire her pearl earrings, which matched her white blouse. Her gray suit seemed out of place at "The Hot One" coffee shop. Turquoise removed her suit jacket and placed it on the back of her chair nonchalantly.

Dakota noticed that Turquoise was not wearing any rings on her fingers — a good sign for this bachelor. After the second hour, Turquoise persistently pursued the unanswered question about Dakota's wink.

Dakota stroked his chin with his right hand as he narrated, "One day, I was saving a deer that was caught in a bear trap. While attempting to free the deer, the bear trap slammed down on my foot and removed two toes."

"Oh, no — how awful!" gasped Turquoise. She stared more deeply into Dakota's black-diamond eyes.

Dakota, not to be sidetracked by Turquoise's inquisitive eyes, returned his own somber gaze.

Dakota continued his tale. "Almost every time I stand up, I feel a wincing pain. Please don't mistake that wink for flirting. But if it got you to come to the coffee shop with me, then good," chuckled Dakota Blackfoot.

After Dakota recounted his hunting accident, he began to unfasten the black bolo tie around his neck. The smooth ebony-leather of his tie matched his wide, antique, western-style Concho belt.

Turquoise secretly admired this tall, irresistible stranger across from her. Gliding her eyes slightly toward the floor, she noticed that Dakota was wearing stone-washed denim jeans with a designer's black leather vest accented with blue-suede pockets. His leather cowboy boots matched his vest. She mentally nodded her approval. His rustic, cowboy shirt blended so warmly with his dark, toasted complexion.

Turquoise concluded to herself, "He looks like a debonair warrior — and a winner."

After three hours, the lively conversation reached its conclusion. "Maybe we can study business concepts sometime together?" Dakota uttered in a matter-of-fact way as he got up from his seat. He winked, and the two of them laughed.

He then handed Turquoise his smartphone, and she proceeded to type in her home and cell-phone numbers. "Yes, that would be nice," nodded Turquoise understandingly, acknowledging silently the pain her new friend felt as he rose to his feet. She recalled his story of losing his two toes and almost his life. It reminded her of that dreadful day in New York traffic.

He insisted on seeing her home, but Turquoise shook her head in protest. She suddenly remembered the promise she'd made to call Ms. Knowing-Feather.

"I have to do one thing before we leave," insisted Turquoise as she stood up from the table and put on her gray suit jacket. She walked to the old public telephone booth, located in the rear of the coffee shop near the restrooms.

Where do I begin? she questioned herself. Turquoise pulled out the letter from her favorite gray pocketbook. She quickly unfolded the letter. She dialed (505) 600-1444 with more than a little conviction and urgency.

Away from the prying eyes and ears of her new friend, Turquoise's heart pulsated wildly. She waited for the phone to be picked up. There was no answer.

On the third ring, Turquoise momentarily daydreamed about her hoped-for success at college. She broadly grinned as she thought about her new life in New Mexico. *Managed Care, compliments of my parents … with an "F" in my business course? It sounds like I need a lot more care in managing my time,* declared Turquoise to herself silently.

The telephone rang for the fourth time. Destiny stepped in and turned another page of Turquoise's life.

"Hello, it's me, Turquoise Nez Timerhorn. Can we meet sooner than we planned?" After her conversation with Ms. Knowing-Feather concluded, she wondered how meeting Mrs. Windsong's relative might change her life.

As they left the coffee shop together, Dakota smelled Turquoise's sweet, exotic perfume and inquired, "What is the name of the perfume you are wearing?" Laughing, she told him, "Surprise me with a bottle of it on my birthday — it's called 'Jeanine.'"

Smiling to himself, Dakota admired Turquoise's youthful bronze beauty. Stimulated by the nurturing side of himself, he wanted to encourage in her the professional disposition he knew she wanted for herself.

Yeah — I'll show her the ropes of mastering time, Dakota empathized quietly to himself.

Holding back his usual assertive approach, Dakota wondered if he could ever win her heart. The bottle of perfume would be one of many surprises he planned for this young lady with the sweeping smile and the forget-me-not personality.

37

Time for the Truth

Sleep eluded Turquoise. She woke up in a cold sweat. At last, she hopped out of bed. Turning on the lamp, Turquoise picked up the telephone and dialed a familiar number.

"Hi, Turquoise — darling, why aren't you sleeping?" came the vibrant New York City voice on the other end of the line.

"How did you know it was me, Mom?" inquired Turquoise, knowing full well that her mother began her day before sunrise.

"Why aren't you sleeping, honey? It's about 2:00 a.m. Mountain Time, isn't it?" asked Teal Timerhorn as only a mother could know when her child was in distress.

"Mom, I keep waking up — the clocks are chasing me. Big clocks, small clocks, even alarm clocks are all running after me," Turquoise complained in a trailing voice. "It's becoming a horrible nightmare."

"Did something happen at school today?" interrogated her mother.

Carrying the portable telephone outside the bedroom so as not to disturb her sleeping husband, Teal Timerhorn reflected on her last conversation with her sister, Sophie Mae. She had told Teal that Turquoise had found the solution for her lateness habit. However, that was in September. The fact that her daughter's success with being on time was short-lived hadn't surprised her mother.

It was only October 10th. Less than four weeks into college, and Turquoise was begging for support. This did not surprise her mother. In fact, it reaffirmed the reasons she and her husband Roy had sent her away for college. It was time for the truth.

Turquoise recounted her most recent class experience. She omitted the part about the coffee date with Dakota Blackfoot, her new male friend.

"Can you imagine, Mom? The professor gave me a grade of 55 on my presentation about time management." Turquoise exhaled and blew off some steam as she recalled receiving that failing grade in her business class. "The audacity of her," began Turquoise's litany of excuses.

Her mother, two time zones away, finished her daughter's statement. It was a whiplash of chastisement.

"The nerve of *you*!" scolded Mrs. Timerhorn. "Arriving late to your college presentation, Turquoise? You have to master time, or you will become enslaved by it."

Realizing that her voice had risen two octaves, Teal Timerhorn softened her tone. She continued in a sage voice, "You can't turn back the hands of time, Turquoise."

"I know, Mommy. I know. I'm going for counseling. I have an appointment next Monday."

Unable to hold back her own excitement and curiosity, Teal asked her daughter, "Will you be taking the trail to Many Farms, Arizona?"

"Yes. How did you know, mother?" asked a puzzled Turquoise.

"I know that the trip will probably take the better part of four hours, so you might need to make a few stops before you reach Many Farms."

Without any further explanation, Teal hung up the phone. Teal mused to herself, *After all, aren't we paying for her long distance calls to New York?* She returned to bed, grateful that Sabera had referred Turquoise to Ms. Knowing-Feather.

Still unable to sleep after speaking with her mother, Turquoise turned around and gazed at the layer of dust on the windowsill. She quietly took a tissue and wiped it away. Suddenly, she rediscovered the silver necklace with the turquoise stone in it. Turquoise dusted around the once-treasured piece of jewelry that her former boyfriend Edward had given her.

The necklace had been left there ever since Turquoise had received Becky's letter. Now, over a week later, the necklace on the windowsill had gathered even more dust. It made the pain easier to forget.

She lay across her bed. It was 4:57 a.m. Mountain Standard Time. Turquoise finally drifted off into a deep sleep. Assuaging her guilt in her clock dreams, Turquoise made plans to change her life.

"My lateness caused me to lose Edward's love. My lateness caused me to get my first failing grade. I jeopardized my friendships back east."

While Turquoise was tossing and turning in her bed, Dakota stirred beneath his heavy brown and white comforter. He felt the coolness of the air conditioner. He, too, was dreaming.

Dakota woke up exactly at 5:05 a.m., around the time Turquoise was falling back to sleep. In another hour, he had to get up. He turned on his right side and tucked the pillowcase under his cheek. He smiled as he drifted back into a light slumber.

Dakota dreamt of her bright brown eyes, her New York City accent that was woven into a basket of intelligence, elegance, and irresistible charm. He searched for a delicate word for her lateness habit. He decided on the word "vulnerability." She was a real woman, one to love ... and to be loved ... but just not the way she was now.

A hip-hop tune began to play in Dakota's dream, and his mental alarm clock went off. He suddenly tossed the sheets off his warm body and jumped out of bed. Dakota Blackfoot rose early each morning without the aid of an alarm clock. He rarely slept past 5:45 a.m.

Anything for You!

Across the room, Turquoise's alarm chimed out. The halogen lamp went on. Turquoise's disheveled hair was spread all across the pillow. It was six-thirty in the morning. A groggy Turquoise stirred momentarily and then continued dozing until she suddenly woke up in a panic. Turquoise bounded out of bed, her heart pounding in trepidation. Meanwhile, she recalled the awful scene of her recent late arrival to class. Now fully alert, she switched into high gear.

Turquoise rushed around the apartment, getting ready for school. She arrived early to class that morning at 7:50 a.m. for her 8:00 a.m. Business class. This morning, at The Sierra Real University, Turquoise had a chance to see Dakota Blackfoot in action.

The showstopper marveled at the showstopper.

It was Turquoise's turn to observe the masterful Mr. Blackfoot at his best. She recognized that he curiously displayed the same charm on the classroom audience that he had shown her yesterday.

His usual attire of jeans and cowboy boots were not in evidence today. He was dressed in a three-piece, dark-gray Italian suit, a white shirt, and a tie with a Southwestern motif on it. Dakota Blackfoot's 5' 11" physique moved effortlessly across the lecture-hall floor as he spoke and made eye contact with his audience.

Dakota, a man from a legacy of winners, was going to college to earn a degree and hopefully meet a woman who might become his life partner and to whom he would discreetly disclose his family's wealth and real estate holdings only after the relationship was firmly established.

From start to finish, Dakota mesmerized his audience, as well as Professor Ackerman. He received a "95" on his outstanding presentation. A true gentleman, he had not failed to utilize all of the training from this course, having fully projected a very professional demeanor.

After the Business class, Turquoise complimented Dakota: "Boy, you were really good! Congratulations on your presentation. What grade did you earn?"

"95," Dakota modestly answered.

"How did you pull that off?"

Instantly processing Turquoise's question, Dakota's empathetic instinct heightened.

"Now, Turquoise, you know perfectly well how I did it. Your presentation could have easily been spectacular, too. However, the delay at the beginning and some errors in logic that arose from your tardiness worked against you, as you likely already know." Dakota said sincerely. He wanted to avoid reminding his new female friend directly that she had been unwisely late to class the day of her presentation.

Just for a second, Turquoise stared into Dakota's eyes. They were, indeed, like ebony diamonds staring back at her with a strength and determination she greatly admired. Dakota searched Turquoise's face for a sign of affection.

Breaking the silence a minute later, Turquoise cautiously asked, "Dakota, I wonder if you would do me a favor?"

"Anything!"

"Could you drive me to Many Farms, Arizona, early next Monday morning? It's close to Canyon de Chelly. I have an appointment there," confided Turquoise. "Are you free?" she queried.

"Sure. We can start on Monday morning at seven and make better time traveling. That way, we won't have to rush."

"By the way, Dakota, my aunt will need to come with us."

Dakota tried to conceal his disappointment at not having Turquoise all to himself for the long-distance drive from New Mexico to Arizona. Nevertheless, Dakota gave her an affectionate wink.

"Thanks for being a good friend," Turquoise responded. Her foremost thoughts were focused on pursuing the prize of punctuality. *Will being a punctual person help me to lead a successful life and, hopefully, regain what I have lost?*

THE JOURNEY ENDURES

(PART III)

39

Apprehension

On that early Monday morning, Dakota, Aunt Sophie Mae, and Turquoise started their journey to Arizona. While Dakota drove from Albuquerque, New Mexico, to Many Farms, Arizona, they had several light conversations.

Dakota was a perfect gentleman as he entertained Turquoise and her aunt with the rich history and folklore of the Southwest. Aunt Sophie Mae often nodded appreciatively in affirmation of Dakota's obvious familiarity with the local culture. Turquoise listened wholeheartedly to his stories as they traveled the countryside of red-clay hills. Nevertheless, her mind kept drifting back to her upcoming meeting with Ms. Knowing-Feather. It had preoccupied her for weeks now.

The threesome arrived at Many Farms, Arizona later that afternoon, greeted by a gracious woman. Turquoise had concealed her concern about punctuality and was quiet during much of their journey.

Circumstances prevented me from arriving on time for class,
Turquoise had repeated to herself, reciting her now-familiar
signature excuse.

Eva Knowing-Feather was Sabera Windsong's cousin. She
was a woman of great wisdom and held the keys that could
unlock many mysteries for Turquoise, who had remained silent
during most of the meal conversation.

After a meal together, Dakota rose from the dining-room
table. He walked toward the front door.

"Thanks for driving us here, Dakota," Turquoise said as
she waved good-bye to him while standing at the door. "See
you on campus," added Turquoise with a more confident voice.

"Do you want me to pick you up and drive you back to
New Mexico?" questioned a concerned, yet eager Dakota.

"No, thank you. Uncle Charlie will come and get us,"
replied Turquoise.

Turquoise lingered at the front door and waved to Dakota
as he walked backward to his car, smiling at her. He raced
off, leaving a smoky trail of red dust behind. Dakota drove
to one of his family's several homes. It was only a few miles
away, in the elite suburb of Sunny Rosa Mesa. Dakota wondered whether remaining silent about his financial status was
wise — in the long run.

With her gaze still fixed on the distant horizon, Turquoise
heard Eva Knowing-Feather say, "Come inside, my child —
let's talk."

The next morning at breakfast, after the introductory
evening conversation with Ms. Knowing-Feather, excuses
poured forth. "I'm sorry," murmured Turquoise, casting her

gaze downward toward the highly polished wooden floor. In an effort to avoid Eva's eyes, Turquoise looked at her Aunt Sophie Mae, sitting across the kitchen table.

"I'm really sorry that I did not contact you earlier, Ms. Knowing-Feather," commented Turquoise as she now stared directly into the mesmerizing eyes of the woman known for her great wisdom.

Eva quickly replied to Turquoise, "That's not necessary, dear. We have much work to do here."

Directing her attention to Sophie Mae, she requested, "Please, enjoy my sunny kitchen; have another cup of tea, and continue reading your magazines."

Rising from the tall, hard-back kitchen chairs, Eva Knowing-Feather ushered Turquoise into her living room. Aunt Sophie Mae flipped through a magazine or two while she patiently waited in the kitchen, where rich, warm rays of sun flooded in through a skylight.

Eva invited Turquoise to sit down on a sofa in the living room — or "conversation room," as Eva liked to call it. A magnificent, glass-top table complemented the mahogany wooden floors.

Eva listened carefully to the troubled young woman as she told her story. "My brother Matthew Creek calls me 'un-lady like' when I rush. He says that people can hear me running down the street to catch lost time." Eva nodded understandingly, without speaking any words.

"I was fired from my job, I lost my boyfriend, I'm failing my first college class, and I'm losing friends because ..." repeated Turquoise like she was delivering a litany. She paused for a minute. The earthquake of emotions she was feeling erupted into a concluding confession: "I am always late." Turquoise wept bitterly.

Eva Knowing-Feather gave Turquoise a box of tissues from the glass-top table. Visible under the table was a valuable, eighteenth-century, Southwestern hand-woven rug. It had been handed down in Eva's family for generations.

As Turquoise dried her tears, she admired the contrast of colors in the rug that were mingled into geometric patterns. The carpet had been created by talented Native American rug weavers. Turquoise had finally ceased talking.

Turquoise caught her breath. She was calmer after telling her woeful story to Eva.

Intent on encouraging her, Eva patted Turquoise's shoulder. "Don't worry. I will help you to help yourself," proclaimed Eva Knowing-Feather. Turquoise remained on the leather sofa while the wise woman rose to her feet.

Eva walked briskly to the window. She searched for the best way to pass on her knowledge. Eva admired the clear blue sky. With her sharp eyes, she saw a bird of prey soaring in the distance, just beyond the mountain range.

A bald eagle, which is an endangered species, is soaring across the sky. One of a kind ... one endangered species in the air and one in danger who is sitting in my living room, thought Eva to herself. She turned away from the window and faced Turquoise with silent determination. Eva returned to her seat on the sofa.

Eva was a woman of few words. But she possessed an effective plan to heal her guest's broken heart. She fixed her eyes on Turquoise while she sat on the sofa.

Eva Knowing-Feather's sympathetic face was etched with wrinkled, sun-darkened skin on her sturdy 5' 1" frame.

"As we talk together, Turquoise, kindle your heart with a burning desire to develop an understanding of the obstacles that hinder your success and how to overcome them," Eva advised.

Continuing, Eva asked, "What do you see as your major obstacles?"

Immediately, Turquoise responded with what she thought was the obvious answer. "My time management is a disaster, and it is hurting my life in so many ways."

"When your alarm goes off in the morning what do you do?" inquired Eva.

"I push the snooze button several times each morning before I eventually get out of bed," responded Turquoise.

"Why do you push the snooze button rather than getting ready to meet the world for a fresh, new day?"

Turquoise was silently reflective but unable to respond. Finally, she admitted, "Ms. Knowing-Feather, I don't know," as she quickly reached for a tissue to catch the tears welling up in her eyes.

"Obviously, you have strong emotions about getting started in the morning. Is your comforter so cozy that it makes you totally unable to put your feet on the floor?" Eva teased kindly.

Turquoise smiled broadly and giggled, "With the way my life has been going lately, staying in bed often feels safer."

"I can readily understand how you might feel that way," Eva affirmed. "But does avoiding life by cocooning yourself in bed resolve your present dilemma?"

"No," asserted Turquoise. "It just makes me begin my day late. Plus it causes me to feel rushed and anxious from there on."

"So once you're late for the bus in the morning," Eva probed, "what excuse do you first tell yourself? 'It took too long for me to choose my clothes' *or* 'I stayed in bed too long'?"

Turquoise thoughtfully responded, "I think I would say 'the choosing of my clothes' or 'doing my hair,' rather than 'I stayed in bed.'"

"Think about all those excuses that you have told yourself and others. Did you ever once admit to yourself that your lateness was under your own control and choice?"

"Yes, I never thought about it in this way before," Turquoise began. "But I am starting to see that I set my own day up for lateness and the stress that follows."

Upon hearing Eva's wisdom, Turquoise realized, for the first time, that she had made herself a nervous wreck, and the complications didn't look good to her. She saw better why she had been sent to New Mexico and to Ms. Knowing-Feather's home. The message and the messenger had evoked the glimmerings of an epiphany.

40

Understanding

The next morning, Eva commented further to Turquoise and Sophie Mae Moon on the décor of her four-bedroom home. Living history could be seen on all the walls, rich with Southwestern patterns, colors, and designs. The tour gave the guests and hostess a relaxed time to get to know each other better.

Afterward, the lessons between mentor and student continued. "From now on, you will begin to see things differently," casually stated Eva Knowing-Feather to Turquoise.

"When a person sees how they contribute to their own difficulties, the changes needed to make their life better come easily.

"The habit of being reliable can be measured by how you fulfill your commitments to others or, in other words, by simply being there at the appointed or promised time. Each person has a universal social contract with all fellow human beings to respect them by being on time." Eva paused and then concluded, "Sunrise and sunset are the larger reality of every individual self."

Turquoise asked, "Ms. Knowing-Feather, please explain further why you used the word 'contract' to describe reliability and commitment to others."

Recognizing Turquoise's interest in business, this gave Eva the opening to clarify. "This contract is an implicit social agreement to value not just the time of others but respect their lives as being just as important as your own. That makes you reliable and committed to both yourself and others as equals. The sun rises and sets on everyone the same."

Turquoise's eyes brightened with perception, "I didn't realize until now how much I was making both myself and others miserable by the way I managed my time. I must promise to respect others and thereby remove the stress on everyone, including myself. It's not just about obligation — it's about mutual happiness. What a great time Edward and I could have had at the prom if I had only lived up to this time contract. Edward did his part. I let him down."

At this point, Eva whispered assertively into Turquoise's ear, "You will not use the word 'late' anymore when you refer to yourself. Negative language tends to reinforce negative behavior."

For a moment, Turquoise was drawn toward Eva's experienced eyes. She felt understood!

Turquoise sighed as she appreciated the huge apricot sun sinking slowly down behind the mountain range. Her light-brown eyes soaked in the beauty and wonder of the approaching sunset. She thought to herself, *This is for everyone.* She remembered and then paraphrased what her father had told her when she was a child: *The eternal odyssey of the sun crosses the sky and blesses the limitless nations who prosper on our lands.* Ancient wisdom and Earth's perpetual beauty now seemed indistinguishable to Turquoise.

41

Early Running Eagle

The next day, Turquoise rose before 5:30 a.m. for her morning meeting with Eva at 8:00 a.m. This was rare for her, since she usually waited until 7:30 a.m. or even the last minute before hurriedly getting out of bed.

"A new day with a new outlook," she told herself.

Turquoise threw the sheets off herself, got up, and then made the bed. She took a shower, brushed her teeth, and got dressed. She combed her hair and left the room at 7:35 a.m.

Eva greeted Turquoise with an approving nod as her mentee arrived early for their morning instruction.

After breakfast in the "conversation" room, Turquoise slid her fingers softly against the wool rug hanging on the south wall of the room. Eva pointed out to her two guests proudly, "It is a rug woven by my ancestors and passed down to me."

Eva shifted the focus of the conversation.

"Turquoise, our lives are very much like the threads of this rug that attracts you so much."

"How is that?" inquired Turquoise.

"I'm going to allow you two to continue your conversation," Sophie Mae interjected and left for the garden outside.

Now that they were alone, Eva responded to Turquoise's question.

"Each thread in the rug can represent an individual. As all of the threads are interwoven together, you see the whole rug — the tapestry is like a society."

"How does that relate to my lateness problem?"

"We, as members of our modern society, do follow certain universal rules such as courtesy to one another and being on time to show respect. However, our contemporary culture has also encouraged harmful self-preoccupation."

"What would happen if I removed one thread from this rug, Turquoise?"

Turquoise spent a moment weighing the options then rejoined, "It would destroy the beauty of the rug. It would disrupt the flow of the pattern in the design and possibly even cause the rug to unravel."

"When you choose to see the rug only as a collection of individual threads, rather than a woven whole, you render its beauty superfluous."

"Oh, my. I am just now realizing that this was what I was doing, Ms. Knowing-Feather. Each thread does its part to make the rug a beautiful whole. I need to uphold my part. And I will! Thank you so much for pointing this all out to me."

This interchange between hostess and guest continued until the last few warm sun rays filtered into the living room through the windows.

On the third day of instruction, Turquoise was sitting at an enormous round wooden table in Eva's kitchen. It was the final day of teaching by the elder woman who was Ed's mother's cousin.

Turquoise was an engaged listener to Eva's words, which Turquoise considered precious drops of water nurturing her parched brain. Turquoise gained strength from them.

"Our tradition teaches us that words have power for both good and ill. We choose words carefully," Eva pointed out. While Eva sipped her hot tea from a baked-clay cup, Turquoise focused attentively on her final day of apprenticeship.

"Remember — never use the word 'late' again when talking about yourself," Eva Knowing-Feather emphatically repeated to Turquoise twice.

In a solemn tone barely above a whisper, Eva Knowing-Feather authoritatively informed Turquoise, "The final key to your puzzle is that you will need a new name that fits your new identity as a punctual person."

Refraining from tasting her hot, buttered corn muffin, resting on a plate, a startled Turquoise frowned and asked, "Uh, a new name, Ms. Knowing-Feather? I have a fine name already! I am Turquoise Nez Timerhorn," she asserted to her advisor.

At just that instant, the sun's rays pierced through Eva's parted kitchen curtains. The rays warmed Turquoise's face as she turned to wait for Eva's answer.

"From this day on, you will be known as 'Early Running Eagle,'" declared Eva Knowing-Feather.

Catching her breath before going on, Eva continued, "The more you use the word 'early,' the more you will become early." Eva directed her words of wisdom to Turquoise who was in the process of a transformation.

Turquoise realized that she no longer had to be crippled by lateness. She accepted her new name. Early Running Eagle had awakened.

Love and Architecture

Ed Windsong picked up Stephanie Strong from her home, and they headed out to a new worksite.

As she got into the car, she remarked to Ed, "On time, as usual."

After Stephanie snapped on her seatbelt and settled in, she observed, "We've been seeing each other quite regularly these past few months, and I have come to really appreciate our common interests in carpentry and affordable housing."

"I very much agree with you, Steph," said Ed as he reflected. "Our discussions about Donated Dwellings and our work with them make the two of us ideal partners."

"I wanted to share with you more about the door-installation project you hooked me up with," Ed continued. "It reminded me so much of the great time I had with Mr. Timerhorn, when we put in his new front door. You would love its Southwest Mission style. Setting it in place impressed upon me the skill it takes to make a door fit correctly in its frame. I can't imagine a better hobby, if you want to call it that. It also jibes perfectly with our college schedules. What more could you ask for?"

Stephanie smiled demurely and added, "A future architect, me, and a future lawyer, you. There's no limit to what we can do, together."

She eagerly followed with an accolade to her admiration of the Arts and Crafts style. "Don't you just love those cute bungalows that were so popular back in the twenties and thirties? Wouldn't it be fun if you and I could invest in restoring one of them and selling it?"

"Hmmm," mused Ed with a glint in his eye. "I'm not so sure that I would want to sell it."

Pulling into the worksite, they tabled this conversation for later.

"See you for lunch at twelve-thirty?" Stephanie queried.

"Absolutely!" Ed confirmed.

A few weeks later, Ed stopped by a local jewelry store to browse. He asked himself, *Where would we live? We both need to attend college for three more years. Am I ready? Is she truly right for me?*

43

I'm Going with You

Turquoise (a.k.a. Early Running Eagle) had returned with her Aunt Sophie Mae and Uncle Charles in mid-October to Albuquerque, New Mexico, from Arizona. She was equipped with a plan of action: *on time means pacing with time — not racing against it.*

Like soaring eagle wings, she tenaciously pursued the Punctuality Prize daily. Eva Knowing-Feather had given her the gift of putting the puzzle together. However, Turquoise would win the precious prize of Punctuality only if she could be both persistent and consistent.

Turquoise returned home to New York for Thanksgiving. At the dinner table, she announced, "Guys, I'm doing better in school."

"That's great." Teal asserted.

"We are both so proud of you," her father added to the conversation.

However, three months later, Turquoise had to admit to herself that she still had a ways to go. But she had been late only twice to college since her "enlightenment." She was glad that she hadn't shared her new name with her family at Thanksgiving because she was not yet completely "Early Running Eagle."

Turquoise received her transcript at the end of her first freshman college semester. She was not disappointed. Holding her fall transcript in her hand, she sighed, *M–m–m — all A-pluses and only one unfortunate C in my Business class. I guess Professor Ackerman saw the timely improvement in me,* chuckled Turquoise to herself.

After the Spring semester of her freshman year, on an early June morning, the phone rang. Turquoise lifted the telephone receiver next to her bed and asked drowsily, "Who is this?"

"I'm sorry to wake you up," sobbed a voice, "but my father was just rushed to the hospital. I wanted to talk to a friend." The long-distance caller continued, "I know it's too much to ask of you, Turquoise, but ..." whimpered the soft voice, as moans trailed off from the telephone.

"What? What?" asked Turquoise, patiently.

"Could you please come to New York?" pleaded the female voice over the telephone. Jane Best, sitting outside of an intensive care unit of a New York City hospital, wiped the anxious tears from her face. Jane waited for the doctors to return with news of her father's condition. Since her mother had died in childbirth, he was the only parent she had ever known.

Turquoise interjected forcefully, "Say no more, Jane. I will be there on the next available flight." She swiftly hung up the telephone, so grateful for the way Jane had empathized with her personal struggles over those many prior months. *How could she not be there, with Jane, in her time of need?* Especially after she was there for me during my emotional breakdown after hearing from Becky that Ed had moved on. Rather than allowing me to indulge in my self-pity, she encouraged me to participate in school activities. There was always some new fun venture to get involved in. Slowly, I realized that she was a great friend. I only hoped that one day I would be able to return the favor.

Then she immediately called her new friend. The male voice that she had come to admire and rely on answered at 2:04 a.m.

Dakota read his caller ID, picked up the phone, and said in a groggy voice, "Hello?"

"Dakota, can you drive me to the airport, now? I need to fly immediately to New York. Jane has a family emergency," Turquoise explained.

"Can you be ready in twenty minutes?" inquired the tall, charming bachelor who had, in his own way, secretly grown to love and admire Turquoise ... from afar.

"I'll be waiting for you in my lobby," Early Running Eagle stated emphatically.

She packed a small overnight bag speedily, having learned the fine art of punctuality by this time. Allowing her natural beauty to shine, she decided that applying make-up was a nonessential that she could do without at the moment.

Nevertheless, there was one thing that she couldn't do without — the now-dusty, silver-and-turquoise necklace on the windowsill. It had lain undisturbed for months.

Since I'll be in New York ... I might just need it, Turquoise nonchalantly thought. She picked up the necklace that Ed had given her and dropped it into her overnight bag, along with a few other articles of clothing.

As she locked the apartment door of 2A and descended the one flight to the lobby, she reminded herself by repeating the following words, "Time to be a winner. It's a zip."

With five minutes to spare, Turquoise took a rapid inventory of her progress since meeting with her mentor, Eva Knowing-Feather.

The old me was too noisy and would talk forever to anyone in sight and on site. I bet I must have scared a few people at times by speaking to them without a proper introduction.

While waiting for Dakota, she approached the mirror in the lobby. Turquoise examined her appearance.

While I'm in New York, I'll treat myself to a new hairstyle, she thought.

Looking around to make sure that she was alone, her thoughts became audible. "I am no longer 'Turquoise.' I am 'Early Running Eagle.'" An expansive power of change had set in. "I will have to make it clear to all of my friends and family who I am now."

A minute later, Dakota Blackfoot pulled up in his customized, shiny, black, four-wheel-drive vehicle designed by his uncle. Ever since he'd met Turquoise, Dakota had been successful in concealing from her that he was heir to a fabulous gem-mining fortune in three western states.

Young Mr. Blackfoot lived in a modest apartment, where he did his own laundry and cleaned without any assistance. However, the car he drove couldn't be found in any car dealership, unless you belonged to the privileged class. The Blackfoot family owned both small and large international companies. Their net worth from the mining industry and real estate exceeded the budgets of many small towns on the east coast of America.

"Money has never fazed me, and it will never break me," Dakota told his father one day when he was only sixteen years old. Years later, at the tender age of nineteen, Dakota had already started his own timepiece firm, D. Blackfoot & Company. He had learned the fine art of business negotiation from his parents. Starting his own company seemed sensible as well as profitable for a young man who was trying to find his own financial niche.

While other teenagers were out on the football field, Dakota enjoyed learning to run his own business. He used the precious stones from his family's domestic and international mines to design unusual watches for all types of achievers in life. Dakota thought he was accustomed to dealing with gems.

Dakota had never expected to meet a young woman who could captivate him by her mere presence. But recently, he had met Turquoise Nez Timerhorn, a rare gem herself. Yes, she did have a tiny flaw, but he had assured himself that this would not affect their relationship; he would make sure of it.

As usual, Dakota was on time, but so was Early Running Eagle. He saw a ravishing young woman in a flowing white blouse over a form-fitting denim jean skirt. The ivory heels accentuated her bronze showgirl legs. Dakota mused, *How many people would notice that Turquoise has a very slight gap between her upper two front teeth? Yet, that's what makes her smile so endearing.*

"How long have you been waiting?" Dakota asked his special new friend.

"Not long. Just two minutes," Early Running Eagle proudly stated. She had learned from Eva Knowing-Feather the power of words.

Dakota pulled away from the Alta Mesa Apartment Complex. They sped to the airport. While Early Running Eagle filled him in on the emergency, he made a mental note of an apparently significant change. Before, Dakota had taken Turquoise's casual attitude toward being on time in stride. He was spellbound by her intelligence, beauty, distinctive smile — and, now, by her punctuality. *Perhaps, I need to think about Turquoise more deeply*, Dakota pondered.

Early Running Eagle interrupted Dakota's thoughts by saying, "Thank you so much for coming to my rescue once again with your offer of transportation and support. I know it must be an imposition, but you know how much Jane's friendship means to me. She has stood by me from the start. I can't possibly fail to be there for her right now."

Dakota gently intruded to ask, "How is Jane's father doing? Have you had an update?"

"Not really," Early Running Eagle answered, "but I hope that his condition has stabilized."

"That would be a relief," Dakota assured her. "Jane is such a fine and interesting person. I like her down-to-earth quality, especially for an executive's daughter. No hint of snobbery."

Changing the subject, Early Running Eagle confided, "I want to share my experience with you."

"What are you referring to?"

"Do you remember when you drove my aunt and me to Ms. Knowing-Feather's home in Arizona?"

"I sure do." Dakota smiled as he recalled spending the night at his home in Sunny Rosa Mesa, near Ms. Knowing-Feather's.

"Well, the outcome of my visit is that I have assumed a new name."

"But you have a lovely name."

Early Running Eagle chuckled, "At first, I responded in the same way. However, in the future, I plan to use the name 'Turquoise' for legal purposes only."

"What should I call you, then?"

"'Early Running Eagle.'"

"Okay, if that is what you prefer. I guess it's not a problem. It's a perfectly traditional name and so fitting for the lovely Southwest setting around us. But I'm curious to know how and why you settled on this name."

"I'll share that tale with you later; however, going forward, please call me 'Early Running Eagle.'"

Minutes later, Dakota and Early Running Eagle arrived at the airport. Her slender hand opened the car door commando-style, barely waiting for Dakota to come to a full stop. With her large, black-leather pocketbook over one shoulder and carrying a small overnight bag in the other hand, Early Running Eagle jumped out of the car. She landed on her feet like a cat.

Speaking over her left shoulder, while starting to run toward the terminal, Early Running Eagle said in a breathless voice, "Thanks so much for the ride, Da–ko–ta."

After quickly parking his vehicle in the parking lot, Dakota Blackfoot pursued Early Running Eagle. He protested, by blurting out, "Wait, I'm coming with you. W-A-I-T!"

"What?" yelled Early Running Eagle. Regrettably, she couldn't hear him clearly because there was an airplane soaring into the sky above them. The ascending plane flew over these two shouting friends.

After the plane had reached its altitude and was inaudible, Dakota lowered his voice. He moved closer and put his arm around Early Running Eagle's shoulder. "Don't rush off so fast, Early Running Eagle."

"If you *didn't* want me to go, why did you drive me here?" Early Running Eagle asked coyly. "What's on your mind?" she inquired.

"I can borrow my company's jet where I work, if I make a call. I want to come with you. Jane is my friend, too! Yes?"

"Yeah, Jane is your friend, also." Early Running Eagle was realizing for the first time that Jane and Dakota had a friendship in their own right.

"Well, don't just stand there, Dakota. Make that call," quipped Early Running Eagle gratefully.

Dakota rushed Early Running Eagle to the terminal reserved for private planes. She waited anxiously as Dakota temporarily left her. He winked back at her. She knew that this was his special way of reassuring her. He winced only when he sat down or stood up, she reminded herself.

A minute later, Dakota picked up the red telephone receiver to set up a flight plan for the company's private jet to leave immediately. Dakota fleetingly thought to himself, *I'm on my way from New Mexico to New York City. My eagle is in flight. Will I still be, or can I be, a formidable contender for her affection there as well?*

44

It's a Small World

Five minutes later, Dakota returned and informed Early Running Eagle that they would be taking a private flight directly to Kennedy Airport.

He revealed that he had permission to use the company's private jet. Dakota's explanation for flying to New York in the style of the rich and famous barely registered with Early Running Eagle. She was clearly more concerned about arriving on the East Coast in the fastest way possible. The stunning couple boarded the sleek private jet. For a fleeting moment, she noticed that the interior of the airplane mirrored the quality in Dakota's customized car.

Several hours later, Dakota and Early Running Eagle arrived and entered an exclusive private room in a New York City hospital. Jane was surprised by Early Running Eagle's miraculously quick appearance in her father's room. Caught off guard, she dropped a plastic bottle of water on the floor when she saw her friend's face hesitantly peering into the room. Dakota followed behind Early Running Eagle.

Jane smiled briefly at the young man beside Early Running Eagle. She knew well those deep-set, sparkling eyes. Dakota approached Jane, took her hands, and offered her a comforting hug.

"Thank you both for coming so soon," Jane softly exclaimed and then embraced Early Running Eagle, her friend from New Mexico. "Wow, you have traveled like the speed of light to New York to be at my side. Thanks so much."

"Thank you for coming to be with my daughter," commented Mr. Best. Talking with obvious discomfort, he added, "Jane has been telling me about the wonderful changes you have been able to make in your life."

Flustered, Early Running Eagle replied, "Yes — thank you, sir. How nice of you to care ... especially at this time.

"How are you feeling now?" Early Running Eagle inquired respectfully.

"A little better, however, I still have to do some physical therapy before I'm released from the hospital, Turquoise. It's important to be proactive concerning your health."

"Dad, please rest now — and no more speeches," Jane interrupted.

"Let me share this good news with you, Mr. Best and Jane. You happened to mention the word 'proactive.' Well, I have taken on a personal challenge to get ahead in life. Please call me by my new name that I am using, which is 'Early Running Eagle.'"

"Really, Ms. Timerhorn?" Mr. Best tried to sit up in the bed upon hearing this announcement.

"I'm glad for you, Turquoise — oh, I mean, 'Early Running Eagle.' I like your new name because it reveals that you are the one who will arrive first," Jane said as she gave the thumbs-up sign for encouragement.

A moment later, Mr. Best revealed to his guest and daughter, "One of my assistants will be stopping in to see me in a minute. I have to sign some urgent contracts. Business never waits. I will introduce him to you," the CEO of Best Pharmaceutical Company commented pleasantly to his former employee, whom he had reluctantly dismissed due to her excessive lateness.

Pushing himself further up on the inclined bed, Mr. Best acknowledged Dakota's presence.

"Excuse my manners, Mr. Best," Early Running Eagle apologized. "This is Dakota Blackfoot, my friend. He kindly offered to come with me on this visit. Dakota, this is Mr. Best, Jane's father."

"Blackfoot, Blackfoot?" Mr. Best repeated aloud as he tried to recollect where he had heard the name before. "Is your father's first name 'William,' by any chance?"

"Why, yes, Mr. Best. How do you happen to know my father?" Dakota replied.

"Dakota, my brother, Daniel, has mentioned your family over the years as thriving entrepreneurs."

"O-o-o-h — your two families know each other?" Early Running Eagle asked, not waiting for Dakota to respond.

Deliberately evading his friend's comment, Dakota first replied to Mr. Best's revelation. "What a coincidence, sir. Please allow me to wish you a speedy recovery."

Before Early Running Eagle had a chance to discover exactly how Dakota's family knew a wealthy tycoon like Mr. Best, the door to the hospital room swung open. Mr. Best's assistant had arrived, and their visit concluded with a mutually grateful, "See you later."

45

Surprise After Surprise

Preparing to leave the jewelry store at 10:30 a.m. on Wednesday, Stephanie commented, "Ed, thanks for letting me pick out my engagement ring. The solitaire diamond resembles a perfect rose growing through a platinum lattice."

Ed, in a rare moment, impulsively fell to one knee and repeated the words he had spoken three weeks earlier: "Stephanie Nicole Strong, will you do me the honor of spending the rest of your life with me?"

Stephanie beamed radiantly and offered her hand to help lift Ed to his feet. He gallantly kissed the back of her hand. "Yes," she whispered.

"Ed, I'm so excited about our engagement party," exclaimed Stephanie. "Believe it or not, this will be the fanciest affair that I have ever experienced. My prom wasn't much to speak of. My date was a really nice guy, but we were just friends.

This, Ed — it's for both of us. I'm so grateful to my parents for going the extra mile. I hope you don't think this is too extravagant."

"No, Stephanie, it's not. I'm going to love it, and so will everyone else."

Meanwhile, across town, another couple — Early Running Eagle and Dakota — were exiting the New York City hospital. They walked briskly toward a waiting town car. At the very same moment, one of those infamous bike messengers whizzed past. The biker stopped abruptly and looked back in disbelief at the passengers who were entering the town car.

Was that who I thought it was? Griffin Lee Browne questioned himself. *"Is Turquoise back?"* he exclaimed. Continuing his reverie, he thought, *Ed's engaged, and now it's time for me to make my move. I'm going to return Turquoise's wrist watch and, hopefully, see if she will go out with me.*

Forty-five minutes later, the town car pulled up to the Timerhorn home. Dakota leaned over to Early Running Eagle and said, "I would love for you to have dinner with me tomorrow night, if you're available."

"I certainly should be available, since my parents don't even know that I'm home yet. They're going to be doubly surprised. I would like to introduce you to them before we return to New Mexico, together."

Pleasantly taken aback at Early Running Eagle's apparent recognition of their relationship, Dakota concluded "I'm very much looking forward to our dinner tomorrow. And I can't wait to meet your parents. Is it okay if I pick you up at 6:00 p.m.?

I'm staying at a corporate apartment in Manhattan." Early Running Eagle affirmatively responded with a nod.

"*Carpe diem*," Early Running Eagle replied as she winked, blew a kiss, pivoted, smoothly slid across the seat, and exited the car. While standing in front of the door of her home, before putting her key in the lock, she wondered silently to herself, *how can Dakota be staying at a corporate apartment in Manhattan? What kind of company does he work for? I will have to find out about this mystery — and soon.*

Early Running Eagle unlocked her front door and yelled, "Surprise, everyone — I'm home!" The unexpected visitor was joyfully greeted by her siblings and parents, who all were relaxing in the living room.

"What's new, Turquoise?" Rita asked with great curiosity, since she had enjoyed the solitude she'd experienced because her younger sister was away at college.

"I want to share this announcement with the whole family, Rita — not just with you. Mom and Dad, please sit down for a second. Matthew Creek, stop playing your video games," requested Early Running Eagle.

"Don't tell me you bought another clock!" joked Matthew Creek.

"No, and stop trying to be funny, Matt. I have learned the importance of being on time. This means not arriving at 1:00 p.m. if you have an appointment at that time. This means that you should arrive at least fifteen minutes earlier so that you are indeed on time for this one o'clock appointment. By being there at 12:45 p.m., you allow yourself sufficient time for a missed bus or a delayed train."

Teal and Roy glanced at each other and smiled.

"Did they teach you this at school?" asked Matthew Creek.

"Are you just now realizing that it is inconsiderate and disrespectful when a person is late, Turquoise?" asked Rita, who had had to wait for her sister on many occasions because she wasn't ready for a party. Therefore, they arrived late and missed a lot of the fun.

"Rita, I have changed. I have a new name, which is 'Early Running Eagle.' Watch me as I live my life differently from before."

"I apologize to you — Rita, Mom and Dad, and, especially, to you, Matthew Creek. I'm sorry that I had overlooked the significance of being on time."

"Apology accepted, Early Running Eagle," Rita said, acknowledging her sister's new name but waiting to find out more.

"Let me share with you some of the knowledge that I have learned while I was away. For example, I no longer schedule back-to-back appointments, and I get up thirty minutes earlier each day. I start my tasks working from a 'to do' list that I create the night before," summarized Early Running Eagle. "I also allow extra time to complete my tasks. I'm so grateful to Ed Windsong's relative, Ms. Knowing-Feather, who counseled me."

Deeply gratified by Early Running Eagle's new found maturity, Teal embraced her daughter tenderly. "Congratulations, Sweetheart," she asserted as she beamed with pride.

"The timing is perfect to share this good news," announced Roy Timerhorn. "You just mentioned your high school friend, Ed. His life has changed, just like yours." Unanticipated words were spoken, and Early Running Eagle's father walked up the stairs to the second floor of their house, joined by her mother.

Early Running Eagle had barely gotten over her amazement at learning about Stephanie and Ed's big engagement party on Saturday from her parents when the doorbell rang.

Roy Timerhorn shouted from upstairs, "Early Running Eagle, please answer the door."

Rising from the loveseat in the living room, Early Running Eagle moseyed to the front door and opened it. Before her stood a dashing man with a large bouquet of pink roses in front of him, blocking his face. He lowered the roses to reveal his identity. Early Running Eagle let out a squeal, "Griffin Lee Browne?"

Stunned, Early Running Eagle blurted, "Uh, uh, P-p-please come in, Griffin."

46

The Best Laid Plans

Griffin and Early Running Eagle took up opposite positions in the living room — Early Running Eagle on the loveseat, Griffin in the easy chair.

"These are for you, Turquoise," Griffin began.

"Thank you, Griffin. Please lay them on the coffee table. I'll take care of them later. By the way, can you address me as 'Early Running Eagle'?"

"Sure, but why?"

"Plain and simple, I have changed since I've been away, and it is my wish that I be called 'Early Running Eagle.'"

"OK, OK. I know better than to argue with a lady."

Flowers were not able to break the tension of this awkward moment. Although there were times that Griffin had walked her home, he had never been invited inside.

"What prompts this surprise visit?" queried Early Running Eagle.

"It's going to be difficult to explain, but here goes. The day you had your near-miss with a Mack truck in the middle of Lexington Avenue, I was there, believe it or not."

Early Running Eagle's eyes widened.

Griffin continued, "I hope you don't hold this against me. I was the one who pushed you to safety and retrieved your watch. I'm sorry it's taken me this long to return it to you or even let you know that I had it. Here's your watch."

"So, Griffin — *you're* my hero!" Early Running Eagle asserted as she accepted her watch with a marked sense of relief and amazement, noticing "D. Blackfoot & Company" on the dial.

"Why did it take you so long to approach me?"

"Early Running Eagle, I was hesitant to ask."

"You, hesitant?" Early Running Eagle interjected honestly.

"I have always felt that I was a bit of a bystander in your life." admitted Griffin. "I always felt you were keeping me at bay when you called me 'your Muffin.'"

Sensing for the first time that Griffin may have harbored a crush on her, Early Running Eagle realized that kindness required her to handle this recognition with tact and empathy.

"I have learned, Griffin, that I need to be more thoughtful about my relationships with others. I truly regret it if I gave you any reason to feel that we were more than just very good friends. I never intended to mislead you, but I see now that I may have, and I'm sorry. That being said, I want to assure you that I am eternally grateful to you for rescuing me. This watch will be a constant reminder of your heroism and a token of our deep friendship."

Early Running Eagle stood up with open arms.

Griffin rose to embrace her. He was noticeably moved. "No one has ever spoken to me this way before. Thank you, Early Running Eagle."

Leaving Early Running Eagle's home, Griffin now rushed to arrive at the restaurant before Valerie. Trying to manage the turmoil in his mind, Griffin almost crashed his car, speeding through an intersection. When Griffin had seen Early Running Eagle earlier that day in Manhattan, he had hastily set up a date by phone with Valerie for 9:00 p.m. His intention was to break up with her after forging a relationship with Early Running Eagle. But, as fate would have it, things had, unfortunately, not gone as planned.

Chez Celeste was one of the more notable French Provençal restaurants in the New York City area. The owner had chosen this Williamsburg neighborhood to highlight its relaxed, rustic fare. Valerie Dewmore loved coming here. The cuisine always presented something tantalizing, but her favorite dish was the lavender-scented Crème Brûlée.

The sights and smells of Valerie's cherished restaurant couldn't take away the dread of this evening. She wished Griffin would have taken the initiative — even if only on one occasion — to plan a special evening for them. She didn't like having to suggest *everything*.

When she had first recognized that the Browne household was missing a mother's touch, she had bent over backward to help out around the home. She volunteered to cook weeknight meals and to do light cleaning. She was gratified that both Griffin and Mr. Browne felt comfortable with her presence and assistance. *If only he had expressed some appreciation,* she thought to herself.

Griffin bounded in the front door of the restaurant, sweaty and out of breath. He had just run two blocks from his parking spot. Valerie was seated in the waiting area of the restaurant and rose to meet him, saying, "What happened, Griffin? You look like you were in an accident."

"Nothing happened, babe. Get our table while I go to the men's room and clean up." Griffin was trying to be as pleasant as he could to Valerie. They had had a few disagreements over the last month, and he didn't want to create a scene tonight. He was now silently hoping he might be able to salvage this relationship, since it was apparent that Early Running Eagle was never going to be his. She had learned the fine art of being on time. Without the liability of being late to pull her down, Early Running Eagle was truly a worthy person to date *or* have as a friend.

Meanwhile, Valerie had finally summoned the strength to end her relationship with Griffin. Originally intrigued by his coarse-but-lovable character, she now found him to be distant, moody and, worse yet, unappreciative of her care. Relationships had to be more than all give and no receive. Valerie, feeling parched, called the waiter to the table. "Please bring two sparkling waters for us." The waiter smiled and quickly went about his task.

Once Griffin returned to their table, Valerie started, "I know that you said you had something important to tell me, but I would like to say something first."

Pausing to gain her resolve, Valerie took a sip of the water and continued, "I wish our relationship was as stunning as the surroundings in this restaurant. For some time now, I've felt that you have taken me completely for granted."

Furrowing his brow in contemplation, Griffin realized that Valerie's accusation was 100 percent true. "Can I say something?" Griffin interrupted.

"Go ahead."

Attempting an apology, Griffin said, "I'm sorry." But he was unable to continue, as his thoughts were in a tailspin. He was unable to express himself further.

"We've been at it for three years, Griffin, and I don't feel that anything will change. It's best that we part as friends now before we cause each other irreparable heartache."

Completely crestfallen, Griffin acknowledged, "I wish it could have been different, Val, but you are probably right about this. I need to rethink the way I handle my relationships with others. If you are willing, may I continue this discussion down the road?"

"There are needs and expectations that must be met in every relationship, but we haven't provided them for each other. I think we both need time for serious reflection."

Momentarily, the waiter approached the table to take their dinner orders. Griffin looked up and said, "Thank you, sir, but I think we're going to leave it at drinks. May I please have the check?"

47

Time to Talk

On Thursday morning, Early Running Eagle was on her way to the New York City hospital to see Jane and Mr. Best. *Adversity can strengthen relationships*, she was thinking to herself. *Whoever would have thought that I would be wishing Mr. Best good health, when he was the person who fired me? And think of the good that has come to me because I had to deal with it honestly. I hope he continues to improve and that Jane's mind will be at ease.*

When Early Running Eagle arrived at Mr. Best's room, he was downstairs at physical therapy, which gave Jane and Early Running Eagle an opportunity to talk privately.

"How are you dealing with the stress of all this, Jane?" Early Running Eagle inquired.

"Dad is recovering quickly, and I feel like my life is coming back," responded Jane. "I want to get in some beach time before we have to return to New Mexico in August. So, how is it that you managed to have the charming Mr. Blackfoot accompany you to New York?"

"Well," Early Running Eagle responded, "Dakota obviously doesn't have to keep the nine-to-five hours most working people do. Any more than that, I can't tell you yet, Jane. But I intend to find out."

"However," Early Running Eagle added, "he doesn't know the details of the very important experience that I had last autumn. Our relationship is definitely a work in progress."

Early Running Eagle spent the next half-hour with Jane relating the effects of her visit with Ms. Knowing-Feather. She concluded by emphasizing, "As a result, I have learned that punctuality is essentially a matter of showing how much you respect the lives of the people around you."

Early Running Eagle then concluded, "Jane, please give your father my best when he returns. Let him know that I will visit tomorrow and every morning until I return to New Mexico. Unfortunately, I have a previously planned lunch appointment for noon today and I must leave now."

Early Running Eagle and Becky had agreed to meet at the Spotlight Diner, where the crew occasionally gathered for burgers and fries.

Early Running Eagle arrived twenty minutes before noon, and Becky got there a few minutes later. Becky promptly eased into the seat across from Early Running Eagle. Flashing her trademark smile, she exclaimed, with a glint in her eyes, "Turquoise, you beat me here; I'm impressed!"

"I know, Becky. Please call me by my new name which is 'Early Running Eagle.' I'll tell you my story in a minute.

Let's not start our conversation before I greet you properly after such a long separation."

They rose together and hugged amicably, swaying and giggling from side to side.

Returning to their seats, Early Running Eagle began by asking Becky how her relationship with Colón Benitez was going. Becky informed her that she and her linguistic buddy from Hawthorne Hills High School were actually planning to accompany Becky's mother on a trip to the Philippines in July. Early Running Eagle found this news absolutely intriguing.

"Looks like we'll both be joining the frequent flyers club," Early Running Eagle responded. "If someone would have told me last year that I would be seeing a young man who could arrange plane trips at a moment's notice, I would have said they were crazy."

Becky exclaimed, "Girl, continue with your story."

"Before I go any further ..." Early Running Eagle paused. "I want to apologize to you for all the times my lack of punctuality gave you the impression that I didn't value you or our friendship. I can only imagine how annoying and frustrating I must have been to you and the rest of the crew. Can you ever forgive me?"

With tears welling up in her eyes, Becky responded gently, "Of course, and I already have. I believe that the person you hurt the most was ultimately yourself."

"Yes," Early Running Eagle confessed. "But it caused me a lot of heartaches before I saw how destructive my behavior had become. Fortunately — and this is something for which I'll be forever grateful — I had the opportunity to engage in some conversations with a very kind and enlightened woman who just happened to be a relative of Ed Windsong. She helped me to view the world not as 'my world' but rather as a shared reality. The old adage, 'Do unto others as you would have others do unto you' really hit home for the first time."

"Wow! Going out west has, remarkably, brought out the best in you, Early Running Eagle," declared Becky.

Early Running Eagle reached across the table. She grasped Becky's hand, smiled modestly, and whispered, "Thanks."

Standing in front of the diner, the two best friends gave each other a good-bye hug and vowed to keep in touch.

"See you Saturday night at the engagement party," Becky shouted as she got into a taxi.

"I'll be there with my family. We were all invited," replied Early Running Eagle.

Early Running Eagle was on her way home to prepare for her dinner date with Dakota. Waiting to cross the street, Early Running Eagle noticed a beautiful sight in the sky. Swerving, gliding, looping, first chasing, then following, these two iridescently breasted pigeons were engaged in a fanciful dance. She was enthralled by their choreography. The freedom of flight invigorated Early Running Eagle.

48

The Big Reveal

No longer than it took Early Running Eagle to walk to the bus stop, her cell phone rang. She immediately recognized Dakota's number. "Hello, Dakota" she intoned. "I'm waiting for the bus to go home."

Dakota was warm but urgent. "Don't get on the bus, whatever you do! I'll pick you up in five minutes. Let's take in a tour of a museum this afternoon. What you're wearing will be fine. We'll keep this day informal."

Flattered by the surprise, Early Running Eagle quipped, "I'm all yours if you can find me!" She chuckled and added, "I'm on the southeast corner of Ninth Avenue and 35th Street."

What seemed like moments later, a sleek black town car eased up to the corner as Dakota opened the back door by the sidewalk. Early Running Eagle hopped in and gave Dakota a quick peck on the cheek. Dakota proceeded to put his arm around her shoulder.

"Early Running Eagle, how about visiting the new Decorative Arts Exhibit at the International Museum of Design uptown?"

"Oooooo, we should be able to view some fine jewelry and ceramics," Early Running Eagle proclaimed.

Dakota responded, "And hopefully some exquisite clocks and enameled bronzes."

Continuing, Dakota said, "Your interest in beautiful jewelry doesn't surprise me, Early Running Eagle; we've often spoken about your preference for fine watches, but I wasn't aware of your attraction to the ceramic arts."

Early Running Eagle enthusiastically responded, "Dakota, I really appreciate our shared interest in the arts. We're not only business-minded but also aesthetically inclined."

As they exited the town car at the museum, they each secretly hoped to unlock the mystery of the other's life. Early Running Eagle was fascinated by their commonalities, but she also had so many unanswered questions about Dakota's background.

Meanwhile, Dakota asked himself, *Could Early Running Eagle ever feel comfortable enough with my family to continue in a relationship with me?*

The decorative arts on exhibit at the museum had been curated into a most innovative collection. Examples of international ceramic art had been carefully selected and grouped to display patterns that were clearly but unexplainably universal. A trio of ceramic bowls, Native American, Asian, and African, mesmerized both Dakota and Early Running Eagle. With a distinctive ovoid shape, each was crafted from a contrasting shade of earthen clay. While the necks of each bowl were of varying lengths and shapes, the design on each was achieved by raised, knobbed, textured, and swirled coils.

Early Running Eagle couldn't hold back her excitement. She exclaimed, "Isn't it amazing how three diverse cultures came up with such similar designs? Each of these would look fabulous on a polished oak table."

Dakota responded empathetically, "Early Running Eagle, I love the moving effect that beauty has on your whole demeanor. I agree with you — it is absolutely transformative."

Considering to himself, Dakota reflected, *I grew up with art like this because my parents could afford it. Early Running Eagle brings such a refreshing perspective, as she has not experienced priceless art outside of a museum. I must assure her and her parents that my family history will never outweigh my care for her.*

Continuing their contemplation of the remarkable exhibit, these two young souls luxuriated in the grandeur of the artifacts and each other's companionship.

Early Running Eagle suddenly felt a gentle rumble in her stomach. "Oh, Dakota, it's almost seven o'clock, and I'm getting hungry. How about you? We have wonderfully lost track of time," Early Running Eagle observed as she gently placed her hand on Dakota's arm.

"You are so right!" Dakota agreed warmly. "We also need to nourish our bodies. Let's find a quiet table over at Chicken Cuisine on 125th Street."

At dinner that evening, over tasty fried chicken wings, potato salad, collard greens, and sweet tea, Early Running

Eagle began to get answers to several nagging questions at the back of her mind.

Dakota was amazingly candid and beguilingly unapologetic. "My paternal grandfather was an outstandingly talented artist in both ceramics and silver. What he was able to do with precious metal and turquoise was in high demand in the midtwentieth century. Not only did he have a dedicated tourist clientele, but he also attracted the attention of a fine jewelry designer from California. The two men formed a collaboration that was to permanently change my grandpa's and our family's lives."

Pausing for a second to reflect, Dakota continued by saying, "Grandpa was in his forties, and the jeweler was in his early seventies. The two men quickly developed a business partnership that led to Grandpa taking over the jewelry company when Mr. Osillios died."

"Is that why I am wearing a D. Blackfoot & Company watch today?"

"You can probably deduce from my story the answers you've been looking for."

"I'm both intrigued and stunned," responded Early Running Eagle. "My first impulse is to say, 'What an amazing business model' — so that's how you were able to get a private jet for us to travel to New York City so quickly, Dakota," summarized Early Running Eagle. "This is going to take me some time to digest. As thoughts occur to me, may I feel free to ask you more questions?"

"Absolutely," Dakota replied. "All this privilege and opportunity was a gift to me. I certainly did not create it. To be honest, I am still trying to sort out all the issues it raises for me. I just wanted to be sure you don't feel that any of this is in any way a barrier to our relationship. Grandpa Blackfoot was just an ordinary man who happened on an unexpected opportunity to better himself and seized it."

Leaning closer to speak into Early Running Eagle's ear, Dakota whispered, "Are you ever going to tell me the reason for your trip to Ms. Knowing-Feather?"

"Well," Early Running Eagle began and proceeded to lay out her misuse of time and the consequences she'd had to pay. How Ms. Knowing-Feather gave her the gift of insight that enabled her to accept the past and change the future. The manifestation of this epiphany was her new name, *Early Running Eagle*.

Arriving back at the Timerhorn home, as they stood on the front porch Dakota gently placed a kiss on her lips.

"Thanks for a wonderful day. I hope you enjoyed it, too," whispered Early Running Eagle as she gently placed a kiss on Dakota's lips.

"I most certainly did! What time would you like me to arrive for dinner tomorrow?" asked Dakota.

"Six o'clock should be just fine."

Giving Early Running Eagle one more hug and a kiss on the cheek, Dakota leaped down the porch stairs and ran to the waiting town car. He hadn't felt this elated in years and wanted to do something notable for her. Dakota had a great idea: *I will make Early Running Eagle know how much I respect her true identity.*

49

I'm on a Mission!

By 9:30 a.m. on Friday, Early Running Eagle was up and out to the hospital, keeping her promise to visit with Jane Best and her father. She found out that Mr. Best would probably be returning home at the beginning of the next week.

Early Running Eagle's dependability over the past week had truly touched Jane's heart. She felt that her initial impression of Early Running Eagle as essentially warm-hearted and sincere had been vindicated by her expression of goodwill during her father's illness.

"Jane, I will do everything possible to stop by again tomorrow, but I can't promise. With the engagement party and my hairdresser appointment, I just may not have the time."

"I understand fully," Jane affirmed.

Mr. Best asserted, "Early Running Eagle, I can't thank you enough for supporting Jane during this critical time of my recovery. I can see how much you value my daughter's friendship, and I am grateful beyond words for this. I will never forget you or your kindness. Plus, your lifestyle change of being a punctual person makes me happy because I see many great opportunities happening in your lifetime."

Giving Jane a quick hug and a double hand clasp to Mr. Best, Early Running Eagle remarked, "I'm not going to say goodbye now; I have a feeling that I will see you tomorrow."

With a dash to the elevator, Early Running Eagle headed to her favorite dress boutique, *Michele's*.

The window of *Michele's* was bursting with the latest summer frocks. Sophisticated, vibrant outfits adorned the mannequins. She remembered the admonition of her father's sister, Aunt Inola: "Elegance is always in season."

Moving through the row of evening dresses, Early Running Eagle happened upon a stunning amethyst dress. Laden with sequins, the dress gently shimmered as it reflected the light. Slipping it on over her head in the fitting room, she was amazed at how urbane she looked. The drape of the dress accentuated her figure, but not ostentatiously. *I have just the right heels to go with this dress. I'll take it*, she thought and proceeded to the checkout counter.

While waiting to pay for the dress, she continued to ponder, *I haven't seen Ed in almost a year. I wonder what kind of gown Stephanie selected for the party. After all, an engagement party is not an ordinary affair. A public commitment like this is not made every day. I hope Ed and Stephanie will be very happy together.*

Walking to the front door, she happened to notice a display of sleeveless frilly blouses. *Normally, I would stop to browse, but not today*, Early Running Eagle thought to herself. *I'm on a mission: Get home and help Mom get ready for Dakota. I want everything to be perfect for this evening.*

With that, Early Running Eagle paid for her dress, left the store and walked to the train. As usual, the train was late. Five minutes passed, then fifteen. Twenty minutes later, the train finally arrived. The conductor made an announcement as the doors were closing. "Sorry for the delay. We have unexpected track work, and the trains are running only every thirty minutes." Early Running Eagle mused, *I'm glad I didn't stop to look at those blouses. I would have been very late if I had.*

Arriving home composed and unfazed by the minor delay, Early Running Eagle bounced into the house and said, "Mom, I'm home. How can I help?"

Teal demonstrated her leadership qualities in how she orchestrated her children to get the home ready for an important guest. It wasn't every day that your child brought home a "special" friend. Teal understood how important this evening was for Early Running Eagle. She instilled in Early Running Eagle's siblings the importance of being at their best, especially to Matthew Creek.

Ten minutes before six o'clock, Dakota pressed the doorbell. While he waited for someone to answer, he admired the craftsmanship of the Timerhorns' front door. *This is exceptionally fine workmanship,* he thought to himself. Dakota was startled as Roy Timerhorn swung the door wide open to invite him in.

"Welcome to our home, Dakota," Roy began.

"Thank you for inviting me, sir." Addressing Mrs. Timerhorn, Dakota said, "Please accept this orchid arrangement as an expression of my gratitude."

"Oh my, Dakota. What a lovely and thoughtful gift. Thank you," Teal softly remarked.

Introductions were made. Teal Timerhorn, Rita, and Early Running Eagle returned to the kitchen while Roy and Matthew Creek entertained Dakota.

"By the way, Mr. Timerhorn, I was admiring the design of your front door. I love the Mission style as well, and that circular window is certainly a unique but entirely complementary feature."

Mr. Timerhorn, appreciating Dakota's kindred eye, smiled brightly and commented, "None of the models available fully satisfied me. So, I chose the one I liked best and added some custom carvings and inlaid it myself. Then I refinished it to take on the look you presently see."

"What an innovative solution!" Dakota replied.

Roy Timerhorn and Dakota Blackfoot spent the next half-hour before dinner engagingly exploring their common artistic passions.

At dinner, sixteen-year-old Matthew Creek was noticeably fascinated with Dakota's presence. He waited for the right lull in the conversation to field his big inquiry. "Dakota," Matthew Creek began, "Early Running Eagle told me that you own a plane. Can you take me flying sometime?"

"If it's okay with your parents," Dakota responded as he looked at Mr. and Mrs. Timerhorn in the eyes with a wink. "I'll be happy to take you for a quick spin around the area the next time I'm in New York."

"Awesome," Matthew Creek gleefully exclaimed, extending both of his thumbs upward.

Matthew Creek had managed to steal the show that evening. Meanwhile, the earlier discussion around the dinner table had bridged some understandable distances and expected concerns among the Timerhorns and their guest. Roy and Teal Timerhorn were pleasantly reassured that Early Running Eagle had met an honorable young man in Dakota Blackfoot.

As Dakota lingered over his good-byes that evening, Early Running Eagle felt relief. The week had started with distress but was now ending in contentment. Her good friend's father was on the mend and she'd had a wonderful catch-up with her best friend, Becky. The smiles on her family's faces revealed their approval and acceptance of her new young man and best of all, she was feeling a closeness to Dakota that was refreshingly sublime.

50

Already in Flight

Early Running Eagle awoke early on Saturday morning rested and full of exhilaration from the night before. "No matter what, I must get a short visit in with Jane and her father before I leave tomorrow."

Leaving the hospital for the last time, Early Running Eagle reflected on how this week had had a reoccurring pattern to it. First, visit Mr. Best and Jane; then, take care of personal business; and finally, Dakota.

The train was on time, for a change. Early Running Eagle marveled that she would arrive for her appointment thirty minutes early. Nevertheless, she had prepared beforehand and had left home extra early.

At ten o'clock on the same morning in June, Margaret Blazer was checking her hairdresser's appointment book. She noticed a name that she had seen before: "Turquoise

Timerhorn." The appointment was for 11:00 a.m. "She's going to be late, as usual. I hope I can fit her in," sighed Margaret.

The doors of Margaret Blazer's Hair Salon swung open at 10:25 a.m. "Hi, I'm your 11:00 a.m. appointment," said a 5' 7" figure in cowboy boots. She was wearing a form-fitting pair of jeans with a sleeveless blouse.

Margaret scrutinized her early arrival closely. *Could this be Turquoise? Little Miss Lateness is arriving early? There's a story behind this that I've just got to hear,* thought Margaret to herself.

Exclaiming in joy, "It's y-o-u, Turquoise!" Margaret twirled around near her front desk and stepped backward to view the stunning young lady who had just entered her hair salon.

"Hello, Margaret," Early Running Eagle said modestly.

As Margaret began to cut and style her hair, Early Running Eagle offered a sincere apology for the numerous times she'd been woefully late for her appointments. She shared with Margaret the punctuality workshops that she had experienced with Ms. Knowing-Feather and the background of her new name.

While paying for her services, Early Running Eagle again thanked Margaret for the great hairstyle she had fashioned and for accepting her apologies.

Margaret replied, "You're welcome, Early Running Eagle. Now you will have that fresh look to match the updated you."

With that, Early Running Eagle went home to prepare for the evening.

As Roy looked outside the window of their second story bedroom he said to Teal, "The limousine has arrived." The

Timerhorns had graciously accepted Dakota's offer to pick them up and take the family to the engagement party. Dakota had wanted to thank them again for their hospitality on the evening before.

"Let it be, Roy. Adjust your bow-tie. You look so handsome in that tuxedo," commented Teal.

Giving her a big hug Roy smiled back at Teal and said, "No, you're the ravishing one this evening."

"Aren't you forgetting something?" Teal inquired as she gave Roy a gentle peck on the lips.

"What, honey?"

"Remember, at our daughter's graduation, you said that you would reveal to me what happened on the stage with Principal Tuftmarks the next time you wore a tuxedo?'

"You have a remarkable memory. One week prior to the graduation I had a meeting with Principal Tuftmarks and asked her to deliver a private message to our daughter." As Roy reflected on that meeting he hadn't realized that he had paused the conversation.

Teal inquired, "And the message was … ?"

Roy responded, "Time to change in order to reach your full potential, Ms. Timerhorn." He continued, "I knew I had to intervene after the disaster at the prom."

"Well, it worked!" Teal acknowledged.

"Yes, Teal, we can be confident that Early Running Eagle will live up to her name now."

Exiting the bedroom Roy and Teal gently squeezed each other's hand as they went downstairs to join their guests and children.

"Let's get this show on the road!" Roy smiled. And with that everyone exited the home.

The limousine was well-appointed with every amenity. Matthew Creek was tickled to no end that his favorite sparkling water was in plentiful supply.

The Dusty Rose Pavilion was all aglow. A million tiny lights strung through the trees made it reminiscent of entering a fairytale castle.

Oh, my, Teal thought to herself as they arrived in the limousine. *Sabera had told me that Stephanie's parents were planning a very elegant affair. But I didn't expect it to be this grand.*

Entering the beige marble lobby of the reception area, the Timerhorn family and their two male guests were astonished at the shine, sparkle, and detail.

"I've heard of this place on the East River," Early Running Eagle commented. "But this exceeds my expectations. I can't wait to catch a glimpse of one of the bridges."

Taking the whole entrance in view, Dakota was mesmerized, quietly nodding his head in approval. The gifts from the members of the Timerhorn family were appropriately placed on the elaborate receiving table overseen by an alert attendant.

Next the guests were greeted by first the Strong parents, then the Windsong parents, and finally Stephanie and Ed. Stephanie was absolutely stunning in her vintage 1930s satin gown. The texture of the gown glistened under the fluorescent lights. Ed was exceptionally handsome in his modern tuxedo with the satin Nehru collar.

Each family member in turn gave their well wishes to the Strongs and Windsongs. As Early Running Eagle and Dakota approached Ed and Stephanie, Early Running Eagle felt a flutter in her tummy. The only other time she had ever experienced this sensation was speaking at graduation before the entire student body. She was surprised at her reaction. Utilizing her breathing technique from yoga, Early Running Eagle slowed her breathing down and, with it, the butterflies in her stomach.

With a heartwarming smile, Early Running Eagle began the introductions, "Congratulations to you both on your engagement. Ed Windsong, Stephanie Strong, I would like to introduce my friend Dakota Blackfoot."

Stephanie reached out and gave Early Running Eagle a big hug. "It is nice to finally meet you," she announced. A little startled, but unruffled Early Running Eagle said, "Nice to meet you, too."

Firmly grasping each other's hands, Dakota and Ed exchanged pleasantries.

"How long will you be in New York?" queried Ed.

Dakota, answering for the couple said, "We're leaving tomorrow morning."

Early Running Eagle added, "But we'll contact you and Stephanie the next time we're in town. Maybe we can meet for dinner?"

The etiquette requirements having been completed, Early Running Eagle and Dakota joined the rest of the Timerhorn family at their assigned table.

The seventy-five guests had found their appointed seating. The gathering included a most diverse crowd. The several families closest to the Windsongs and the Strongs were seated in a semicircular row around the platform where Ed and

Stephanie would shortly announce their engagement. Then, in the second row, were the friends Ed and Stephanie had met during their first year of college and their volunteer work. In the outer row sat the few high school friends that Ed and Stephanie still kept in fairly close touch with. The chamber music quartet had modulated their concerto to completion.

Mr. and Mrs. Windsong and Ed ascended to the platform from the right, while Mr. and Mrs. Strong accompanied Stephanie from the left. The parents, first the Strongs and then the Windsongs, graciously thanked the guests for coming. Continuing, the parents addressed Ed and Stephanie individually, formally acknowledging their relationship in warm and endearing terms. They shared both serious and humorous anecdotes about this new couple that thoroughly engaged the audience.

Stepping down and taking their seats again, the parents left Ed and Stephanie on the platform alone. Ed briefly shared the ordinary but charming way he had reconnected with Stephanie. Likewise, Stephanie related her initial feelings about second chances and Ed.

The guests were so moved by their narrative that when Ed bowed on one knee before Stephanie, they didn't know whether to applaud or say *"Oooooooo."* There was a little of both.

Ed waited for silence before proceeding. "Stephanie," he began. "I simply couldn't wait for another three years to pass to ask you to spend the rest of your life with me. I know that we have committed to completing college before our marriage. However, I wanted very much to let you know now that I love you."

Taking the ring box from his inner vest pocket, he slowly opened it, revealing a sparkling solitaire diamond ring chosen by them earlier. As Stephanie extended her left hand, Ed gently slipped it on her ring finger. Rising to his feet, Ed smiled mysteriously at Stephanie.

"Ed????" Stephanie began.

"Stephanie, I have an additional token of my love that I would like to give you." With that, Ed pulled a small, light-blue box from his inner jacket pocket. Opening it, he retrieved a silver necklace which had several thin strands with one large, black onyx gem as the centerpiece and a delicate inlay of amethyst and turquoise stones. The necklace had been passed down in the Windsong family from father to son for generations to share with their wives.

Turquoise smiled to herself, happy that the beautiful necklace was where it belonged on the graceful neck of Ed's future wife.

Speechless, Stephanie hugged Ed tightly. Then, she planted a passionate kiss on his lips. She whispered in his ear, "Now, I am truly a Windsong!"

Taking their place at the small dinner table for two at the base of the platform, the Strong and Windsong parents came up to congratulate their children.

As Sabera hugged Ed, she whispered in his ear, "When did you get the necklace back from Turquoise?"

Ed replied, "She's not 'Turquoise' any longer, Mom."

"Well then, who is she?"

"She's 'Early Running Eagle' and a true champion."

"Why do you say this, son?"

"She returned the family heirloom necklace to me discreetly in the lobby just before we entered for the ceremony and quickly told me about her new identity."

"Returning the necklace was surely timely, Ed. Don't you agree?"

"Yes, I really was able to surprise Stephanie with it this evening."

"I must remember to thank Eva."

"Why, Mom?"

"Never mind, you don't need to know everything, Ed. Enjoy your engagement party. Now, go!"

Mother and son departed after this discussion. Sabera joined her husband, Ben, at their table.

At the end of the announcements an informal receiving line formed as guests came forward to congratulate the engaged couple. The repast was consumed joyfully by all. Finally, after four hours the engagement event ended and the participants departed the pavilion.

The next morning, as sunlight filtered through the kitchen curtains, preparations were being made for a visitor. He arrived promptly at eleven o'clock for brunch at the Timerhorn's house. Dakota felt comfortable to be in these surroundings. As the midday meal and the conversation both wound down, Dakota decided to take the lull in activities as an opportunity to place Early Running Eagle's luggage in the waiting town car which was outside.

Early Running Eagle lovingly squeezed her parents as tears welled up in her eyes. "I don't want to leave. I miss you all so much."

Roy kissed her cheek and said, "The two of you will be just fine. You'll be back for the holidays sooner than you think."

As the car drove away, Teal thought to herself, *I'm so relieved that Dakota and my daughter are taking their relationship slow. I'm happy that they have chosen to finish college first before making any other life choices.*

Arriving at the private jet terminal of the airport, the driver pulled up to the aircraft on the tarmac and quickly opened the passenger door to assist Early Running Eagle and Dakota in exiting.

Dakota abruptly stopped in front of Early Running Eagle, blocking her view of the plane.

Looking up, Early Running Eagle exclaimed, "Aren't we getting on the plane?"

Dakota smiled and retorted, "Yes, but I have a question for you first." Stepping back to reveal a call sign under the pilot's window that read *Early Running Eagle,* he continued, "Let me know when you're ready for your first flying lesson."

"I'm already in flight!" And with that, Early Running Eagle smiled and sashayed up the stairs to board the plane.

About the Author

As a New York State Certified Teacher of English to Speakers of Other Languages (TESOL) and a self-taught expert on being on time, author M. Lauryn Alexander has more than twenty-five years of experience as a classroom teacher in New York City. She has taught all levels of ELL classes in the public high school as well as teaching English to Non-Native Speakers of English on the college level at The City University of New York (CUNY) as an ELL Instructor.

As a teacher, she observed that most students aren't taught time management skills and as a result, failed to see the importance of punctuality in their daily lives. She incorporated time-management topics into her classroom lesson plans. She discovered that the story in her book, *Time & Consequences* was the perfect teaching tool for teens, young adults and adults. In 2017, Ms. Alexander published the novel, *Time & Consequences*.

As a bilingual English/Spanish educator, Ms. M. Lauryn Alexander will be publishing this novel in Spanish in 2024. (www.TimeandConsequences.com)

M. Lauryn Alexander founded Success Essentials Inc.®
(www.EnglishBySE.com), an innovative company that special-
izes in teaching English to English Language Learners (ELL)
and Career Coaching for Advancement™ in the New York
City area. Success Essentials Inc® is an accredited business
with an A+ rating with the Better Business Bureau® (BBB®).

M. Lauryn Alexander is also a member in the New York
City Chapter of the Association for Talent Development
(ATD), the Smithsonian's National Museum of the American
Indian, the Japan Society, and the Association of Publishers
for Special Sales (APSS).

One of her charities that she supports is the American
Cancer Society. Ms. Alexander is a native Brooklynite, as well
as a global citizen. She has traveled worldwide visiting Dubai,
France, Greece and several Spanish-speaking countries such
as Spain, the Dominican Republic, Venezuela, Mexico and
Puerto Rico.

M. Lauryn Alexander hobbies include coin collecting, being a fitness walker and is an avid reader. One of her
favorite expressions that she shares in her Career Coaching
for Advancement™ workshops is the statement, READERS
ARE ACHIEVERS™.

Milton Keynes UK
Ingram Content Group UK Ltd.
UKHW030948140324
439440UK00001B/58

9 780990 758549